My Life as a Mule

My Life as a Mule

Sj Hylton LeHoven

Illustrated
by
Jocelyne Champagne Shiner

Copyright © 2018 Sj Hylton LeHoven

All rights reserved.

www.SjDaisy.com

First Edition

Cover art & design by Jocelyne Champagne Shiner

This book is a work of fiction. Names, characters, businesses, organizations, places, events, and incidents either are the product of the author's imagination or are used fictitiously. Any resemblance to actual persons and/or animals, living or dead, events, or locales is entirely coincidental.

The text of the book is set in 11-point Georgia.

ISBN-10: 0692123059
ISBN-13: 978-0692123058

Dedicated to longtime friends Clarence & Susan.

CONTENTS

The Middle Years CONTINUED – *Still Slightly Damp*

The Later Years – *Almost Dry*

Epilogue

Everybody has begun

their journey of awakening.

Some know it, some don't.

Life is that journey.

Abdy Electriciteh

Interview:
What's It Like to Be a Mule?

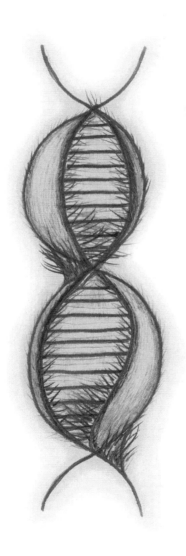

Dear Reader,

Not too long ago, I was interviewed by a high school student, a darling little Mole named Emily. Over and over she asked, "What it's like to be a Mule? And were you surprised to win the prestigious Mathematics Mule of the Year Award?"

I wasn't quite sure how to respond.

So, I decided to answer the second question first. "I was shocked," I truthfully answered, "and honored. To be the first Mule Mare to ever win this award was a great, great honor."

The first question was a little more tricky. I was born a Mule, and I imagine I'll die a Mule, so it's all I know! That got me to thinking. Maybe there are others who also wonder what it's like to be a Mule. I know that I've certainly been curious to know how others live and even wanted to *be* someone other than myself. Like my cute Rabbit friend, Betsy. The clothes she can wear! What looks adorable on her is simply ridiculous on me!

"So what *is* it like to be a Mule?" you ask.

Well, it's probably not that much different from your life.

I was raised in a very traditional family. My parents were right, and everyone else was wrong. Okay, that sounds pretty harsh. Maybe everyone else was *mostly* wrong. But my parents were still always right.

No, they weren't mean to strangers; they were gracious and kind. But underneath that veneer was Judgment. Yes, Judgment with a capital J. I felt Judged all my life. And I Judged. Boy, was I ever a great Judger. I could tell you everything wrong with you. Yes indeedy. Sure, I wasn't perfect either, but I kept myself so busy focusing on others, I didn't see it. That's right. I couldn't see the speck for that stick in my eye.

My birth.

It was in December. I was born. I was happy.

It wasn't until many years later that I put two and two together:

> 1. My dad's birthday was in March.
> 2. My family was broke.

+

> 1. No money for gifts.
> 2. There's a free gift that keeps on giving.
>   *(Well, most of the time.)*

=   Me. Molly, the Mule.

So, now for that interview I mentioned. Enjoy!

What makes you a Mule?

My dad's a Donkey. Okay, he's really an Ass. That's his official title. My mom's a Horse. A very genteel Mare. They got together and voila! Me. A Mule. I have 63 chromosomes. That makes me the odd one.

How many chromosomes do they have?

Dad has 62. Mom 64. One got lost somehow in the making. Or, I was given an extra. It just depends on how you look at it. Such as, maybe the 63 were just to keep me in my place, carefully situated between my parents.

How are you different from your mom? (i.e. a Horse?)

My muscles are smoother. I've got lots more common sense. And I love pizza with mushrooms. She likes hers with sausage.

Do Equines eat meat? Did I say that right? EE-quine.

EE-quine. Eh-quine. Either will get our attention.

Thanks. So do...eh-quines eat meat?

Normally not. But on pizza, it was hard for my mom to resist.

How are you different from your dad? (i.e. a Donkey)

Well, most Mules are bigger than their Donkey dads, but my dad's a Mammoth, so he towers over me.

How tall is he?

56 inches.

And you?

51 inches.

And you call that towering?

Anything more than a millimeter is a tower. It's all a matter of perspective.

How else are you different from your parents?

I'm me. And that's something they'll never be able to do.

Anything else?

Well, I can't reproduce. That means I can't have foals.

Oh, I'm sorry.

It's okay. I've come to peace with it.

Tell us about your ears?

What about them?

Are they different than Horse ears, for example?

Think about it, Emily. If you were to quadruple the size of your mother's ears, what do you think would happen?

I'd be able to hear better?

That's right, Emily. Which can be rather annoying at times. But thank goodness I've had some hearing loss. That really mellowed things for me.

What caused the hearing loss?

Hmm, maybe I should write a book. That would address all these questions.

It would. So why don't you?

Yes, why don't I?

Is there anything else you'd like to add? About how you're different from a Horse?

I'm much stronger than a Horse.

How's that working for you?

Well, it comes in handy to be strong. Except for when I was a foal and it came time to bring in the groceries. Minnie and Marvin never seemed to be around.

Who are they?

Read my book.

So you *are* going to write a book?

Yes, I think I will.

Cool. Who will be in it?

Well, my parents for sure. My dad's name is Jack. Yes, kind of obvious since he's a Jackass, but it suits him. My mom is Sarah. Suits her too. She's a really classic genteel Southern Horse. And a beauty, a real beauty.

How so?

She's a Bay?

A what?

A Bay. She has a reddish-brown coat with a black mane, tail, ear edges and lower legs. Gorgeous.

Would you say that you favor your mother?

Yes. I got most of my looks from my mom.

You mentioned a Minnie and a Marvin?

And I said read my book.

Please, I'm trying to just get some basic facts. Things to help your fans understand your life as a Mule.

My fans?

You have no idea.

Wow, you're right. I don't. And I didn't mean to give you a hard time, Emily. I'm just having fun with you.

That's okay. Any other way you're different from a Horse?

We Mules really do like to socialize. We get along with everyone.

More than Horses?

Yes, more than Horses.

Can you tell me about Minnie and Marvin? Who they are?

Sure. Minnie's my oldest sibling. Also a Mule. She got her name because she's a miniature Mule, a whopping 49" tall. She never let me forget it. "Molly, your ears are SO big," she used to say. "Too bad you're not a miniature like me. Then you could wear cute hats like these." Stuff like that.

How much older?

Minnie's four years older. Marvin two. Just enough to be annoying and helpful.

In what way?

Which? Annoying or helpful?

You just shared an annoying thing about your sister. How is she helpful?

She keeps an eye on me. Always. Used to drive me nuts until that time she kept me from getting kicked by a Mammoth Donkey friend of Dad's. Apparently, he didn't see me, but Minnie did. Called out just in the nick of time.

Nice. A helpful big sister.

Yes, most of the time.

And Marvin?

He's alright. He doesn't rub it in that he's a Dun, like Minnie does.

A what?

A Dun. That's when a Mule gets this beautiful, dark line down their back. Something to do with the cross between the Donkey dad and Mare mom. The mix of the colors. But...the thing is, I didn't get one.

Does that bother you?

It used to but not anymore. I've come to peace with it.

You've said that twice. 'Come to peace with.' How'd that happen?

Well...for that, you'll definitely have to read my book. It was a process.

It didn't happen overnight?

No, definitely not.

So...how will I recognize Minnie or Marvin?

It really comes down to that line. Minnie and I look a lot alike. All that's missing is the dark, dun line.

So, she's a beautiful reddish color like you? With the dark mane and dark lower legs?

That's right.

How about Marvin?

He's a Silver Bay Dun. That means his coat is lighter due to Dad's classic gray. Some may call it champagne, though I think that's much too dressy of a word for Marvin. Tan suits him better. He's tan with Mom's dark mane and tail. And then of course there's that dark, dun line down his back. And none of us got Dad's white around the eyes or the belly. We consider ourselves lucky.

How's that lucky?

Makes us all much more distinguished. Almost Horse like.

Are you saying it's better to be a Horse?

No, definitely not. It's better to be whatever you are.

So, what was your family life like?

Traditional middle class. My dad had a good job. He was a math professor at the college. He's retired now.

So, was that why you went into mathematics?

Partly. It's kind of a long story.

Got it. And your mom?

She was always a stay-at-home mom. Being a Horse of such fine standing, she wouldn't have put up with having to work a real job. Besides, she was always too busy with all her projects around the house.

Such as?

Such as...matching this with that. Hat with dress. Dress with shoes. Shoes with purse. She even liked the toilet paper to match the décor in the bathroom.

And did it?

Yes. She had an ongoing supply of multi-colored toilet paper on order. Blue for Marvin's bathroom. Pink for Minnie's and mine. We used to love to tease her about it.

Why?

Because she was sensitive. And being kids, we simply liked to tease.

Why was she sensitive?

My mom was an orphan. So, she was hyper-sensitive about all kinds of things. She says that her family, if they were still living, that is, would have disowned her when she married my dad.

Oh?

Mom says they were classic Southern. Genteel. White Gloves. That sort of thing. Snobs, if you ask me, but a mixed-marriage? They're all rolling in their graves, she says. And to think their Sarah would have hybrids ...

As in you?

Yes, we Mules are considered hybrids. But, but something's coming to me. That's not really how it is...I mean, my mom's not exactly right about that.

How so?

I've got to sit with this, Emily. Think it through. Hmm, I do think it'll be good to write a book. Get it down on paper. I'm feeling a little tug on my heart.

Cool. Then I think you definitely should. It's certainly interesting.

Is it?

Yes, it is. And enquiring minds want to know. It's not every day that a Mule writes a confess-all book.

It won't be a confess-all book, Emily. I can promise you that. I think, I think it'll simply be my story. How I broke free from the reins of conditioning.

You've had a sex change?

No...and I don't even know if that's possible.

Then a breed change?

No, definitely not. Just a change of heart.

You had a heart transplant?

No, Emily, I've still got the heart I was born with, but...it's changed. Expanded. After years and years of wanting to please my parents. Be a good little Mule. I finally realized that I had to be myself. Completely. Not who I thought I was supposed to be.

And will your book show that?

I don't know. Time will tell.

Sounds like it's time to get cracking then.

Yes, it's time to get cracking. And Emily? Thank you for helping me realize this. That it's time. I really appreciate that.

My pleasure. And thank you for the interview.

You're very welcome. My pleasure as well.

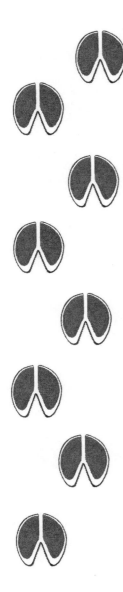

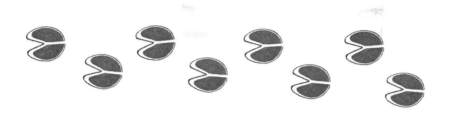

So, after I sat with all this, thought about how to write a book, a friend stepped up to the plate. Agreed to help me. I'd thought being the youngest of three would cover that third person thing, but it didn't. Luckily my friend knows all about that and volunteered to write my story. Not all of it, mind you, just enough tasty bits so that you'll be satisfied without being overstuffed like at Thanksgiving.

I think my friend did a great job.

Enjoy!

Molly
xoxoxo

The Early Years:
Wet Behind the Ears

Not Again
or
Life Skills 101

"Yes, yes, I understand. It won't happen again," said Sarah to Molly's teacher over the phone. "Yes, I understand that students cannot be allowed to bite other students. Yes, yes, I'm so sorry... Oh, please don't pull her out of the program. I've just started something and, well, it just wouldn't be a convenient time...No, Professor McMurdy, I'm not making fun. I understand the seriousness of the matter, but please, sir, please. Give Molly another chance. She just has to stay in the Kindergarten," she pleaded, just barely refraining from saying, it's the last one, I've been through them all!

"Click."

Sarah laid the phone on its cradle. Shook her mane in an attempt to clear her head. It didn't work. She picked the phone back up and dialed. Slowly. She was thinking over what to say to Jack. He was not going to be happy. Of course, she wasn't, but he *really* wasn't going to be happy. All the plans he had already made for Molly. All the graduate schools he had already imagined her attending, trotting in his hoof-steps as a mathematician. All going down the drain. Not even coming out of the tap. Simply evaporating before she'd even left Kindergarten.

"Hello, Miss Barbie," Sarah said to Jack's secretary. "I know he hates to be disturbed, but this is a very pressing matter. It, it has to do with Molly."

Silence. How often has she heard this very same silence from perky little Miss Barbie, a Mouse of a secretary who knew how to maximize every small bit of her cuteness.

"Please," tried Sarah.

Again, silence.

"Oh," said Sarah, desperate to find a solution, "did I mention that a friend of mine returned from Paris last week? She brought a most magnificent wheel of brie. For me. As a gift. And...well, of course I planned on sharing part of it with you, Miss Barbie."

Silence.

"*Cough*. I mean, of course I meant to split it with you," said Sarah.

Even deeper silence.

"I mean, of course I was planning on giving it to Jack to bring in to work tomorrow. I just know you and your family will love it," she said.

"He's right here," Miss Barbie replied so quickly that Sarah wondered if she'd just missed keeping half of that brie. "Darn!" she thought to herself.

"Darn what?" asked Jack.

"Oh," replied Sarah, "I didn't realize I spoke."

"Well, you did. I don't have all day, Sarah. Can't it wait till I get home?" he asked.

"No, Jack, it can't. She's done it again. She's bitten someone at school," said Sarah.

Silence.

"Who? That Billy Goat?" he asked.

"No, thank goodness, not him. We still haven't repaired our front door since that last incident. That father of his is no role model, if you ask me," said Sarah.

"Didn't ask. Well in tarnation, Sarah, are you going to keep beating around the bush? Just spit it out! Who'd she bite this time?" "Betsy, that cute little Bunny."

"Elmer's kid?" Jack asked.

"Yes, Elmer's youngest," said Sarah sadly.

"Good grief, Sarah! What are we going to do with that little Mule! And those teeth of hers! Maybe we can have them re-sized. Or bound like they do with little Mare hooves in China. That's what we'll do. We'll bind her mouth!" he screamed.

"Jack, settle down. We are NOT going to bind Molly's mouth. She has to eat. And breathe. No, we're going to have to take this to someone smart. Someone experienced. Someone..." she said.

"NOT your sister, Martha," said Jack.

"Jack, hear me out. Martha's been really working wonders with some of her students," she said.

"Some of her students, not ALL of her students?" he asked with a ferociousness that meant she'd have to come up with some super-duper way to convince him. "Well, there is that little negligee my friend brought back with the cheese..." she thought to herself.

"Sarah!" Jack yelled. Are you still on the line?"

"Yes, dear," she said. "We'll talk about it when you get home. And oh, Jack, don't hang up. Did I mention that I bought some fresh raw onions from the farmer's market? We can have them on everything tonight. Your favorite. Raw onions pureed on toast. Raw onions over barley. Raw onions and oysters."

"Sarah, if you're trying to butter me up…it's working," he said. "Now bye! I have got to get back to my students."

"Yes, dear," she said just as the phone went click. But not dead.

"Oh, Miss Sarah, I'm so looking forward to tasting that French brie. A whole wheel you said? Don't forget now, you promised," Miss Barbie squeaked in her sickly sweet voice.

"Yes, I'll remember," said Sarah, seething inside. "Oh, that dirty… Mouse," she said to herself. "I've got to figure out how to get back at her!"

"Bam." Sarah slammed the phone onto its holder jiggling the brie which lay close by. "Hmm," she wondered. "How can I take a bite without leaving nary a trace?"

Bible Drill
or
And So It Goes

Molly carefully wrapped her new black Bible in tissue paper. She was so excited to have something new, never before used. "I can't let this get damaged," she thought.

"Hurry up, Molly!" her dad called. "The bus is leaving."

Not that they were really going by bus. The family of five piled into one of their two Beetles, the cute little VW cars that were all the rage. Red and Green theirs were. It was perpetually Christmas at Molly's household.

"I'll be right there!" she replied, carefully tucking her Bible, which she had wrapped in tissue paper, inside a pillowcase. "You can't be too careful," she thought.

Once all the clan had piled into the car, Jack set off. It was the family's weekly ritual to go to church on Wednesday evening. First was dinner in the family dining hall. Then followed different classes for all. Today was extra-special for Molly – her first time for Bible drill...*and* with her own Bible.

After a delicious meal of spaghetti, their mother said, "Hurry along now, girls." Both Molly and Minnie were both in the same class for Bible drill practice. "Where's Marvin going?" asked Molly. "With your father, dear. It's a special meeting just for fathers and sons," her mother explained. "Good," Molly thought, "he won't be able to tease me."

The two Mule Mares dashed off for their practice. Each strategically finding a spot as far from one another as possible. Sharing a bedroom and bed was fine, but sometimes they both needed their space.

"Class! Class!" called out Mrs. Hare. "Time to settle down," she said while carefully holding a tiny stick pin in her tiny Rabbit paw. She stood perfectly still as the class tried to settle down. When the scraping of chairs showed no sign of stopping, she eyed them with her rich brown eyes using the force of her quiet persuasion. Her tall antennae ears rotated from side to side. Gradually, the students began to quiet in earnest.

The newbies were a little curious about that pin. It was a legend in their church that Mrs. Hare used a pin to set a standard of quiet. "What's she going to do?" they wondered. "Stick us if we make a peep?"

Their teacher took charge and said, "Thank you students for settling down. If we're here to learn."

"Doesn't she already know what she's teaching?" Molly wondered.

"If we're to learn," Mrs. Hare repeated, moving her gaze from the front of the class to the back, "then we *all* must be quiet. In my hand, I'm holding a pin."

"Yes," everyone silently agreed.

"I'm going to drop this pin, and I need for all of you to be as quiet as little Sally Mouse," she said. Sally sat up even taller, proud to be recognized. In fact, she sat so tall that her teenie weenie ears almost touched the back of the folding chair.

Just then, Billy scooted his chair just a bit closer. "I can't miss this," he thought. "Ahem," Mrs. Hare coughed, "Billy, are you quite settled? Comfortable? I wouldn't want for you to miss this."

"Yeah, Billy," thought Molly. "Pay attention."

"Yes, Ma'am," Billy coughed.

"Okay students, on the count of three, I'm going to drop this pin. I need for it to be so quiet that all of us, do you hear me?" she asked. "So that all of us can hear it. One, two, three," she said, dropping the pin from her rigidly outstretched paw.

"Ping," heard Molly. "Ping," heard Minnie. "Ping," heard Sally. "Nothing," heard Billy.

"I didn't hear a thing, Mrs. Hare," called Billy from the back of the room. "Alright then, Billy," she said, "come on up front then. Thank you, Sally," she added as Sally graciously crawled down her chair and scooted along the floor back towards Billy's now empty chair. Reluctantly, Billy came forward taking the seat right under Mrs. Hare's nose.

Standing on her platform, she called out again, "Okay, students, settle down. Thank you, Sally. Thank you, Minnie. And now, on the count of three, I'll drop it again. One, two, three," she said.

"Ping," heard Sally from the back of the class. "Ping" heard Minnie. "Ping," heard Molly. "Nothing," again, heard Billy.

But rather than shout this time, Billy used all the restraint he had and slowly raised his front hoof, holding it high. "Yes, Billy," said Mrs. Hare. "I didn't hear it," he said in a tone that challenged his teacher to prove him wrong. "No?" she asked. "You didn't hear a thing, Billy?" "No," he said.

The rest of the class moaned.

"Alright, students," she called. "We're going to give it one more go. Billy" she said, "I want you to lie on the floor. Right here in front of me." He obliged. Billy really wanted to hear the ping.

"One, two, three," she said, again dropping the pin straight down on the floor.

"Ping," heard Minnie. "Ping," heard Molly. "Ping," heard a little Pig sitting in the rear.

"I heard it! I heard it!" shouted Billy, jumping up from the floor.

"Well done, Billy," said Mrs. Hare using her tall ears to push him back down in his chair. "Well done," she then announced to the entire class. "It's time now for Bible drill. Please get your Bibles."

Molly carefully pulled her Bible out from her pillowcase, then gently unwrapped the tissue and placed it back in her cloth bag. Standing at attention, she held her Bible on her outstretched right hoof placing the left on top, mimicking what her older siblings had shown her. "Well done, Molly," said Mrs. Hare as she walked around the room inspecting each student's posture and form.

"I learned from my big sister and brother," Molly said proudly, noticing Minnie's smiling face on the other side of the room.

"Good form," Mrs. Hare said also to Sally, who stood on her chair holding her tiny made-for-a-Mouse Bible.

Once she was certain that all the students were in position with their Bibles carefully resting on their palms, she began. "Now, as you may or may not know, Bible drills are an important part of building your familiarity with the Bible. Good Christians know exactly where each book of the Bible is. Last week we completed the memorization portion of the class with most of you able to recite the books of the Bible in proper order," she said, eyeing Billy. Everyone knew that Billy was the only one not to learn them in proper order.

"These first few times will be practice runs. I'll call out the name of the book of the Bible, the chapter and the verse. You'll open your Bible and as swiftly as possible find the location of the verse. Are there any questions?" she asked.

"Yes, Sally," she said. "And what do we do when we find it?" squeaked Sally.

"Simply stand with your Bible open to the correct page with your eyes gazing on the verse. That will show me that you've found it," their teacher replied.

"And how do you know we found the right verse?" blurted Billy, forgetting to raise a hoof.

"We will have checkers, Billy," she replied, ignoring his rude behavior.

"She would have made me raise my hoof and ask again," thought Molly, noticing that this teacher like so many others had different standards for Billy and boys in general.

Just then, a row of older students came into the classroom and stood alongside one wall.

"Thank you, students," Mrs. Hare said, acknowledging their presence. "We'll give them a few practice runs before you go and check," she told them.

Turning back to the class, she continued, "And for our first practice run, we'll begin with a very simple verse. One I think you'll all know."

A ripple ran through the class as each student stood up tall holding their Bible in position. From the tallest of the tall to the tiniest of the tiny, they all stood at attention. Satisfied that they were ready, Mrs. Hare began, "Genesis 1:1," she said matter-of-factly.

The students frantically opened their Bibles and flipped the few pages to this very first book of the Bible.

"Good," she called out, seeing that everyone, Billy included, had settled and were looking at their Bibles.

"Another easy one," she said, again waiting until everyone was still. "John 3:16," she said.

Again, the students were frantically turning their pages. Some seemed to know exactly where this verse was located while others were strumming the pages as if watching a private animation show.

While waiting for all the students to settle, Mrs. Hare eyed the room, taking notice of who quickly arrived at the correct destination and who had difficulties with this simple verse.

"Okay, students," she called. "now we're going to do it just like for the contest. How you've been doing it, but this time be sure to hold perfectly still once you find it. No talking to your neighbor. No looking to the side. Just focus on the verse. Our helpers," she added, nodding for them to spread throughout the room, "are going to walk around and make sure that you found the right verse. Then, I'll randomly call on one of you to read what you've found."

Standing up straight, Mrs. Hare showed the students that it was time once again to close their Bibles and stand at attention, ready to go once the verse was said.

"Proverbs 22:6," she called out.

The sound of flipping pages filled the room. Snap, Sally was in place. Snap, Minnie. Snap, snap, snap, several students quickly froze. But at the very front of the class pages were turning back and forth with such ferocity that they surely were being torn.

"Billy," Mrs. Hare called out. "Focus. You can do it."

Finally, after the second hand made yet another twirl around the large clock at the front of the room, Billy stopped fumbling.

"Check it," she said to the helper closest to him.

"It's right," the helper said.

"Well done, Billy, and now please read the verse," she said.

"Start children off on the way they should go, and even when they are old they will not turn from it," Billy read.

"Good, Billy. Now who knows how it's to be done during the contest?" she asked.

Minnie shot up a hoof, wanting to show off her knowledge.

"Okay, Minnie, please demonstrate," said Mrs. Hare.

"Proverbs 22, verse 6, Start children off on the way they should go, and even when they are old they will not turn from it," said Minnie.

"Well done, Minnie. Who can explain the difference between Billy's and Minnie's reading?"

Sally's tiny foot shot up.

"Yes, Sally," said Mrs. Hare.

"She said Proverbs 22, verse 6 at the start," said Sally.

"Very good," said Mrs. Hare. "Now who can be even more specific?" she asked.

Excited that she had understood, Molly raised a hoof.

"Yes, Molly," said Mrs. Hare.

"She said the name of the book of the Bible, the chapter number, and then the verse number," said Molly.

"That's right, Molly," said Mrs. Hare.

"Show-off!" said Billy from the front of the class.

Again, Mrs. Hare didn't correct him.

"What?" Molly thought. "He always gets away with stuff."

"Let's do a few more rounds class," said Mrs. Hare. "John 5:29."

Students ruffled the pages of their Bibles. Checks were made. The verse read.

"And come out – those who have done what is good will rise to live, and those who have done what is evil will rise to be condemned."

"Ephesians 6:2."

"'Honor your father and mother' — which is the first commandment with a promise."

"And lastly," Mrs. Hare said, "Ephesians 5:24."

"Billy," asked Mrs. Hare once she saw that a helper had assisted him in finding the verse, "will you read it for us, please?"

"Ephesians 5:24," said Billy. "Now as the church submits to Christ, so also wives should submit to their husbands in everything."

"Thank you, Billy. Very well done," she said. Facing the class, she announced, "We'll continue with this next week and award those who find the verse first. Remember, only three students can enter the city-wide contest." Smiling at Billy, she added, "Class dismissed."

The students hurriedly gathered their Bibles and began to stream out of the classroom. Lagging behind, Molly slowly picked up her Bible from the chair. Instead of carefully wrapping it in tissue paper, she simply dropped it inside the pillowcase. The waded-up tissue she threw in the trash. The special feeling she'd had for her own Bible had already worn off.

"I don't have a chance," she thought sadly. "It's a male's world, after all."

Molly's Father
or
Can a Donkey Beat a Mule?

"I knew I could beat you, Dad! I knew it!" exclaimed Molly proudly. She had just passed her father in a short running race, glad to be with someone who loved her unconditionally. Someone who didn't think girls are inferior to boys.

"Way to go girl!" he called, huffing and puffing and just barely crossing the line Molly had drawn in the dirt. "Great job!" he added.

Molly was so happy to have time with her dad alone. And to be outside, instead of in his workshop with his beloved chess boards. She absolutely glowed.

"But when you're older," he said," and have a boyfriend, you'll let him win, of course."

"Why would I do that?" asked Molly, indignant that her father would make such a suggestion.

"Well, because..." her father stuttered, "because we males like to win, and to lose to a girl, well, that's just something we can't take."

"You took it," said Molly.

"Well, yes, but I'm your father, and you're a Mule, and Donkeys just don't stand a chance against Mules."

"Are you saying I had an unfair advantage?" asked Molly.

"Well, of course you did," he said, changing his tone slightly when he saw how hurt she was. "But you are a great runner. Really, you are."

"Thanks," said Molly, the pleasure of the moment evaporating quicker than rain in a desert."

Ah, kiddo," he said, "I didn't mean to put you down. It's just that, we males like to think our little Mares need us. Even when they're taller, like your mother," he added.

"You're only a Mammoth Donkey," she said, emphasizing Donkey. Molly wanted him to feel some of her pain. "You're not a Horse, Dad. Besides, she's not really that much taller."

"No," her father said, completely missing his daughter's attempt at an insult. "I think she even forgets sometimes that I'm not a Horse," he said proudly.

"Does that matter to you?" she asked, seeing her father for the first time as a stand-alone figure with his own identity.

"Sure it does," he replied. "Horses usually keep to themselves, and Mares are not really known for taking to Donkeys naturally. But you know how it was for your mom."

"No," Molly thought, "I don't."

"Being an orphan and all," he continued, "she got to know a lot of Donkeys at the orphanage."

"She never talks about it," said Molly, really asking her dad to tell her more.

"No?" he said absent mindedly. "Well, I don't know a lot, but I do know that some of her best friends were Donkeys. So when I came along, it really wasn't that big of a deal for her to hang out with me. Want to race again?" he asked, uncomfortable with this topic. Molly's father wasn't really the type inclined to reflect, unless it was how to win at chess.

"Sure," said Molly. "But just so you can't say I have an unfair advantage, why don't you start here?" she said, pointing at a tree. "I'll go back to the main road," now pointing about a mile down the way.

"Whoa!" her dad said. "Feeling pretty confident, aren't you?"

"Yes," Molly grinned. She loved spending time with just her dad. It happened so rarely that she wasn't going to let it end too quickly if she could help it. Besides, she wanted to show him how fast she really was.

"I'll yell when I'm in position," she called, gently trotting down the lane.

"You got it," her dad brayed. "Wow," he said out loud, "I might actually be able to beat her!"

Change Is in the Air
or
A Bean by Any Other Color

"Mom! I know what I'm going to wear to the party!" called Molly from across the field.

"What?" her mother shouted back.

"My favorite overalls. The ones with the yellow daisies."

"Sounds good. But you better be home in time for dinner. No dilly dallying! And don't forget to pick up all those green beans I left by the pump. You got it?"

"Got it," Molly yelled back. "I'll be there way before Dad gets home. I promise."

Picking up her basket Molly walked towards the pump wondering, "Why are green beans green? They could have been pink. Or yellow."

"What are you rambling on about?" said a creepy little voice from down in the hollow.

"Ignore something you don't like, Molly, and it'll go away." Her mother's saying played in her head. Following this advice, she continued her musing, "I don't think I've ever seen a blue bean. There are navy beans. But they're white. Then why call them navy? Do sailors eat them?"

"What are you rambling on about, ole Molly the Mule?" the voice asked.

"Just keep going Molly," she told herself. "You're almost there."

"Stop! I'm talking to you!" it shouted in a tiny big voice.

Picking up her pace, she muttered, "Ignore it. And it'll go away. Ignore it. And it'll go away."

And then, from the corner of her eye, she saw something green shoot through the sky. "A flying green bean?" she wondered.

"Hello," said the voice from somewhere much closer. "Where are you?" asked Molly. And then it hit her, "OMG, it's on my nose!!!! Eeek!" said Molly, shrieking and shaking her head.

"Won't work. I got suction in my toes. Suction in my woes. I'm a suction king I am. I am."

Still shaking, Molly cried, "What are you? And why are you on my nose?"

"How else could I get your attention? Get you to stop and listen?"

"Get off!" she screamed. "I'm going cross-eyed just looking at you."

"That you are. Yes indeedy, didn't know Mules' eyes could go so far in. Now that is interesting. Very, very interesting," it said, intently studying her face.

"Get off!" she screamed again. "Please!"

"Okay, if you're going to be that way about it."

"Off!!!!" said Molly in a flurry of stomping hooves.

And then, in a soft, almost gentle voice, the creature asked, "What's with all the commotion? I got off. You can quit now."

Dizzy, Molly lumbered in a circle suddenly collapsing in a plop. Dust flew, and green beans went a flying.

"Where are you?" Molly asked from where she sat.

"Up here. On the trellis," it called.

Lifting her head as she tested her legs, Molly pulled herself up only to find that she needed to look down.

"Or rather down here," the creature cried.

Finding composure at last, Molly stopped her wiggling. Standing so still that she could feel the flutter of her heart, she thought, "I only see green beans. Vines and vines of green beans." Afraid to scare away whatever it was, now that her curiosity was piqued, she braced herself for whatever might come. "Where are you?" she whispered.

"To your left," it said.

Molly rolled her eyes ever so slightly to the right.

"The other left."

"Darn," she thought. "I thought I had that down."

And as she searched through the beans, she slowly began to focus on something odd. "Is that a tail? And a leg? One, two, three..."

"Four!" it shouted. "Four wonderful legs that can take me anywhere!"

Its color began to change. What was once a green bean with four legs and a tail gradually turned into a brown bean with four legs and a tail.

"What are you?" Molly asked, not really sure she wanted to know.

"I'm Charlie," it said. "Charlie the Chameleon."

"What's a Chameleon?" she asked.

"It's a me!" Charlie answered proudly.

"I've never heard of Chameleons before."

"No? Well, we're everywhere. You just can't see us."

"How'd you do that?" she asked. "Change your color?"

"It's just what I do," he said. "Wanna know how?"

"Yes!" answered Molly excitedly. She could already imagine it. Changing colors to invisible so she could escape her awful teacher, Miss Granger. Or that obnoxious Goat of a bully, Billy.

"All you have to do," it said, "is let me crawl on your back."

"What?" asked Molly. "Why?" She didn't want to be rude, but she also didn't want to let that little fella on her back. "I couldn't keep an eye on him," she thought.

"Because," he simply replied.

"Because why?"

"Because that's how it's done."

"What should I do?" she wondered. "What would Mom do?"

And in a flash, she knew. Her mother would run, run, run all the way home. "Safety first," she thought.

So before that little creature could tempt her further, Molly turned and ran. She didn't care that her mother would scold her for not picking up all the green beans. "She'll be happy to have me home safe and sound," she hoped.

"Wait!" Charlie called. "Where are you going? Don't you want to change colors? Don't you want..."

But Molly was already across the field and almost safely home before this little silly thing could finish his sentence.

"Molly!" her mother cried when a whirlwind arrived at the kitchen door. "What in heavens name has gotten into you?"

"Mom!" Molly cried breathlessly. "You're not going to believe what I saw! A little green bean with four legs. And a tail! Its name is Charlie, and it wanted to crawl on my back!"

"Did it change colors?" asked Molly's mother with a grin.

"Yes," answered Molly. "How'd you know?"

"Because I've seen them too," she said. "They're just Chameleons. They're harmless."

"But it wanted to crawl on my back."

"It did?" her mother asked.

"Yes," said Molly, still panting. "It said I could change colors too, but it had to crawl on my back, and that would be really cool if..."

"Oh Molly," laughed her mother, "he was pulling your leg. He couldn't give you any special powers, make it so you could change colors. He was just wanting a free ride across the field. It takes them forever to walk that far," she explained. "Really?" asked Molly. "Yes," her mother replied, "Really. Now come on in and help me get dinner ready. Your father's going to be here any second. And wash that slime off your face."

The next day, Molly came down with the mumps. Mumps so large that she thought she was going to pop.

"Mom," Molly mumbled, "I don't feel so good."

"No wonder," her mother said. "Your face has swollen to the size of an Alligator." Placing her hoof on Molly's forehead, she gave a sad sigh, "Doesn't look like you'll be going to that party after all. Mumps are highly infectious, and I can't let you get everyone else sick. It's off to bed for you. I'll start the chicken soup."

"Oh!" Molly gasped. "Not Clara!" She loved her pet Chicken.

"Don't worry, Molly. I've got something that tastes just like Chicken."

Afraid of what that might be, she chose not to ask. "Best not to know," she thought as she headed to her room and warm, soft bed.

What Molly didn't know (until she was an adult) was that her mother never cooked meat. Ever. Instead, she disguised things to look like meat. The chicken in this soup? Tofu. The sausage on her pizza? Tofu with ground nuts. Hamburgers? Lentils, potatoes and nuts. "I can't possibly eat any of my friends," her mother often thought. Her life at the orphanage had impacted her in ways Molly never imagined.

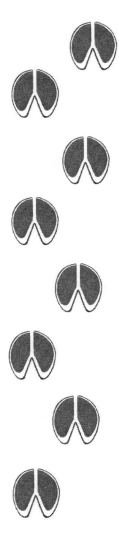

Molly's Mother
or
When in Doubt, Flatter

"You don't know how lucky you are!" screamed Molly's mother.

Not sure how to reply, Molly chose silence.

"You have everything you need. And more. And two parents. Me? My parents died when I was young. I had to live in that orphanage with all those wild animals. You? You need a new outfit, you get it!" she yelled.

Molly didn't bother to correct her. The last time she'd gotten a new piece of clothing was three birthdays ago. Everything else came from Minnie, or the nice Crossley family, who seemed to take pity on her.

"So get in there and clean up your room!" her mother screamed. "Do you hear me?" she demanded.

"How could I not?" wondered Molly, sliding into her room as quickly as possible. Careful not to slam the door and make her mother even madder.

"What is she so mad about?" Molly wondered.

A few hours later, when she realized that she couldn't let go of that question, she decided to go ask her dad. "Okay," she thought, "if I have to suffer through chess for an answer, I will."

"Beats me, kid," was all he said. "She's been like that for as long as I've known her. Sweet. Charming. All smiles. And then the devil itself rises up for a howdy-do just when you least expect it. I suspect it has something to do with life in an orphanage. It couldn't have been easy," he said, his eyes glazing over. He was obviously thinking of things he had better not tell Molly. "She is a kid, after all," he thought.

"So," he said, making an effort to cheer things up a bit, "do your best to stay out of her way. And give her some slack, kid. Use those Mule ears of yours and skedaddle when things get dicey. Now," he said turning to the chess board in front of him, "I'm going to teach you how to take the Pegasus, or Queen like some folk call her."

"I like Pegasus better than Queen, Daddy," said Molly. "And I really like the Mammoth Donkey instead of a King," she added.

"That's my girl," he grinned, "Flattery will get you everywhere."

The Crossley Family
or
Are Hinnies Uncommon?

"Thanks so much for taking care of our garden, Molly," said Mr. Crossley. "The tomatoes would have died if you hadn't watered them."

"You're welcome," she meekly replied.

"And the cantaloupe? Did you enjoy the cantaloupe?" Mrs. Crossley asked.

"Oh," she simply said, not sure what to say. She had also been unsure when to pick it, and it had gone bad. A Rabbit most probably got to it. "Um, it was delicious," she lied.

"Oh, that's so great! I'll have to ask your mother the next time I see her how she enjoyed it," added Mrs. Crossley.

"Oh, she didn't get to have any. We all ate it up so fast, she didn't get any," said Molly hurriedly. The last thing she wanted was for Mrs. Crossley to discover that she had lied.

"A shame. Well, I'm glad you enjoyed it. Thanks again Molly for taking care of our garden. Here, please take this little gift as a token of our appreciation," she said, handing Molly a few coins.

"Oh, I couldn't," she replied, ashamed of her lie. Afraid it was written all over her face. "Maybe that's how tattoos come into being," she wondered silently. "Everyone's secret shame. Felt over and over again until it becomes permanent."

"I insist," added Mrs. Crossley. "Now get on home. I don't want your mother worrying about you."

"Bye, Mrs. Crossley," Molly called as she ran across the tracks. "And thank you, thank you so much for the money!"

"That silly Mare," Mrs. Crossley said, turning to her husband. "Can't tell the truth. Didn't you see that she hadn't eaten the cantaloupe? I bet it turned bad before she even picked it."

"Don't be so hard on her dear," said Mr. Crossley, gently snuggling his wife on the shoulder. "Haven't you noticed how shy she is? How badly she wants to please? It's a wonder she even knows how to be herself, so concerned she is with how others perceive her."

"Yes, dear, I'll try to be more gentle with her. Harriet!" she called, "Why don't you invite Molly over to dinner tonight? I'm making pizza; I hear from her mother that mushroom's her favorite."

"Sure Mom," said Harriet, so deep in her science book that she had not heard a word of her parents' conversation.

"Now, I've got to go to the store to get those ingredients!" said Mrs. Crossley.

"It's for you, Molly!" cried her mother from the other side of the house. "It's that Crossley Mare, Harriet!"

"I'll be right there," yelled Molly back.

Once she had gone downstairs and picked up the extension she called, "Got it Mom! You can hang up the phone."

"Click."

Only after that sound did she speak. "Hey, Harriet, what's up?"

"Mom's making pizza. She said to invite you over."

"Really?" asked Molly, still raw from her recent lie. "Are you sure I wouldn't be an imposition?"

"Nah, Mom loves you. She's always saying, 'You should invite Molly over to play.'"

Silence. Molly wasn't quite sure what to make of that.

"I'm not teasing you, Molly," said Harriet.

"Well, if you're serious," said Molly.

"I am. And get over here quick! I need an assistant for my science project." "Click." Harriet had hung up.

"Mom!" yelled Molly from downstairs, "I'm going to the Crossley's for dinner."

"Now, Molly, dear, what have I told you about being an imposition. They just returned from their vacation. Surely, they don't want another mouth to feed or someone to watch over."

"No," said Molly. "Harriet promised I wouldn't be. Besides, she said that her mom likes having me over," proud to have that little nugget to share.

"You're leaving already?" asked her mother a few minutes later when she heard the bang of the door.

"Harriet needs help on her science project," she called from across the street. Already feeling like she had entered another world. A world where she mattered.

It would be years before Molly would realize that her mother was just voicing her concerns. About mouths to feed. Bodies to look after. And when she got it, it explained so much. Why Molly had felt her mother's resentment at times.

"Others don't really listen to what you say," she would realize one day. "They've already got their opinion based on *their* beliefs, so they just assume you think the same way."

Solving that little riddle would go a long way in helping Molly learn to not care what others thought or said.

"Pizza's ready," called Mrs. Crossley. "Harriet, dear, will you please help Molly set the table? Goodness gracious, I have to ask for your help a thousand times, and Molly just pitches in."

Turning to stick her tongue out at her new friend, Harriet grabbed plates for everyone.

"You only need four, dear," said Mrs. Crossley. "Harry's staying over at a friend's tonight."

"Oh yeah," said Harriet remembering. "The great art project."

"Don't make fun, dear," her mother said, "Harry's really showing some promise in the world of art."

"You're calling that drawing on the fridge art, Mom?" she asked laughing.

"He won an award for it. Something about the way the colors were arranged and complemented each other," she said.

"It's all scientific," added Mr. Crossley, just entering the room.

"For you, Dad," said Harriet, "everything's scientific."

"Well, it is!" he said with glee, rubbing his front hooves together. "The way colors mix and blend. The way the sun sets on the horizon," he said while looking out the window to the distant sun. "And even the way cheese melts and merges with mushrooms," he said, stretching a mushroom up high with a large glob of cheese dripping down.

"Stop that," laughed his wife with a mock pat on his back. "Leave some for the rest of us."

"Yum! Mushroom pizza!" said Molly when she realized what kind it was.

"What other kind is there?" asked Mrs. Crossley with a smile.

"Only because you're here," said Harriet.

"Oh?" asked Molly.

"I do make other kinds," her mother said, "but a little bird told me that mushroom is your favorite," she said, again, with a smile.

"Oh," said Molly, sitting down at the table just as Mrs. Crossley placed the homemade pizza pie on a raised platform in the center of the table. "That's really sweet of you, Mrs. Crossley. Thank you."

"My pleasure, Molly, dear," she said, making sure to make eye contact with Harriet's new friend and science project assistant.

Blushing, Molly looked down where her napkin already lay on her lap.

"Milk?" asked Mrs. Crossley when Molly looked up.

"Sure, I mean, yes," said Molly when her glass was already half full.

"Beer, for me, dear," said Mr. Crossley.

"Already out," she said. "But why don't you pour it, dear. My patience isn't long enough for that to settle."

Grabbing the beer and mug, he came over by Molly. "See?" he said, showing her how he needed to tilt the beer stein just right as he poured the fresh ale into the glass. "Everything is scientific. Even how you pour beer. If I were to leave my glass straight, it'd just be a glass of foam. And how could I drink it then?" he said, laughing and taking a big pull of his frothy beverage. A foam mustache appearing over most of his face.

Molly simply laughed. It felt so good to be at the Crossleys. She didn't really understand why, but somehow as soon as she crossed the railroad tracks, a feeling not unlike the bubbles in Mr. Crossley's beer began to enter her body, rising from her hooves to the top of her tall, tall ears.

"So," said Mr. Crossley, turning his attention now to Harriet who had already piled two slices on her plate, "tell me about this experiment you're working on."

"Oh," said Harriet with a mouth full of pizza, half holding it in her mouth and half blowing. "It's hot!"

"Of course, it is, dear," said her mother, finally joining them all at the table. "Fresh out of the wood stove."

"That's so cool you have a wood stove," said Molly.

"Needed it for a book I was writing," said Mr. Crossley.

"There are wood stoves in science fiction?" asked Molly.

"There was in this one," he said. "Besides, how else could Mrs. Crossley make such perfect pizza. That's one of the beauties of life, Molly. When everything overlaps. Interrelates. Writing a new book," he said, raising his right hoof. "Wanting a wood oven," he said, raising the left. "Voila! Make it so," he said, chuckling to himself.

"Wow," thought Molly. "That's really cool." But all the Crossleys heard was the satisfying sound of a young Mule Mare savoring a big mouthful of fresh, hot pizza.

Focusing now on his daughter rather than his food, he asked, "So, the experiment?"

"We're supposed to measure the speed of trains. So, I just figured how perfect is that! I've got a train track just outside my bedroom practically. Molly was helping me set up some posts. I'm timing how fast it travels from the corner by the stop sign to where the junction is," said Harriet.

"Sounds fun," her father said. "Do you like science too, Molly?" he asked.

"It's alright. What I really like is math," she answered.

"Oh?" he asked. "What do you like about it."

"How it all just works itself out. Like...you can't have something on one side of an equals sign that doesn't add up to the other side. It has to balance," she said.

"Yes, indeedy, that it does," he agreed. "Mrs. Crossley was quite a mathematician in her day, weren't you, dear?"

"Oh, how else can I calculate how best to feed this family," she said, playing down her very obvious skill at managing their small income.

Molly knew that living on the other side of the tracks wasn't considered good by most Mules, at least from the whispering she had heard at church. But it seemed to her that the Crossleys got along just fine.

"They have a great big garden out back," she thought to herself. "And shelves and shelves of food that Mrs. Crossley canned. A beautiful rainbow of food," thinking of the basement shelves Harriet had showed her when they returned from working on the experiment. Jars of tomatoes. Both red and green. Okra. Blueberry jam.

"You could run a store from all you've got in the basement!" said Molly unthinkingly. She hadn't meant to talk out loud and embarrass them. Or herself.

"That we could do," said Mr. Crossley proudly, not at all embarrassed by her outburst. "My wife is a wonder. An absolute wonder."

"Mom?" asked Molly, taking advantage of a rare moment when her mother wasn't occupied with her remodeling. "How is it that the Crossleys are different from us?"

"They're Hinnies," she said matter-of-factly.

"And what's that mean? They're Mules too, aren't they?" she asked.

"Yes," her mother replied. "Technically they're Mules too, but... even *more* technically, they're Hinnies."

Seeing the question mark all over her youngest Mule's face, she explained further. "See, your father is a Donkey, and I'm a Horse Mare, and our babies are Mules," her mother said.

"Okay," said Molly, hoping this wasn't an invitation to talk more about the birds and the bees. "That'd been so embarrassing!" she thought.

"And the Crossleys, well, they're the opposites," she said.

"Opposites?" asked Molly. "Oh!" she gasped, suddenly getting what had been right in front of her nose. "Mrs. Crossley is a Jennet like, like Grandmother."

"No one's like your grandmother," her mother said, again, matter-of-factly. This was a fact so certain, her mother knew that the earth would certainly tilt off its axis if there were ever another being like her mother-in-law.

"No." Molly agreed. "But she *is* a Jennet."

"That she is," her mother confirmed.

"And Mr. Crossley is a Stallion," said Molly.

"Yes, a Horse Stallion. Your brother Marvin is a Mule Stallion."

"Like I'm a Mule Mare," said Molly.

"Yes, you are. A wonderful Mule Mare," she added.

Taking advantage of her mother's unusually good mood, Molly continued, "Okay, so they're Hinnies, and we're Mules."

"Exactly," her mother replied.

"And they're the opposite of you and Daddy," said Molly.

"Polar opposite," said her mother.

Years later, Molly would finally understand what her mother meant by polar opposite. Respect. Mr. and Mrs. Crossley treated each other with mutual respect. They were so at peace with themselves that they didn't need to take their anger out on each other. Put another down to bring themselves up.

"So," said Molly, "if there are a lot of Horses in the world and Donkeys, then why aren't there more Hinnies?"

"Because, well, because it's so difficult for Jennets to get pregnant by Horse Stallions." She too was hoping that this wasn't leading to another conversation on the birds and the bees. She had privately celebrated the completion of that awkward task. Thankful that Molly was her youngest, and she had fulfilled her motherly duty.

Molly sat with this for a moment.

"Was it difficult for you and Daddy?"

"No," her mother laughed. "Your father jokes that by the time I realized what caused me to have foals, you were already teething," sharing the most personal bit of information she ever had with her daughter.

"But, if it's difficult..." asked Molly, not really sure what she wanted to ask.

"Then most Horse Stallions won't put up with that nonsense," said her mother, rescuing her from her own confusion. "But Mr. Crossley is different," her mother sighed. "The scuttlebutt is that he was so in love with Mrs. Crossley that he was willing to adopt if need be. Imagine that!" she said, seemingly forgetting that she was talking to a daughter and not one of her Mare friends, "Being so in love you'd be willing to adopt. Not caring whether you were able to pass on your name or not. Molly, dear," she said, turning and looking her daughter directly in the eyes, "if you ever find someone who loves you that much, snatch him up. Snatch him up right then and there, because I tell you, that is a rare breed. Anyone who can love you so unconditionally."

And as her mother turned back to her magazines, piles of possible re-design plans for their home, Molly felt the wall go back up. Once again, her mother was her mother.

Molly's
Grandma Rose
or
What We Cannot See

Punching the pillow, Molly turned yet again.

"Is this night ever going to end?" asked Molly, trying to get her pillow to fit just right. Trying to relax. Wanting so desperately to sleep.

"Thank goodness Minnie's at that slumber party tonight. I can just imagine the grief she would be giving me."

"Ummph!" Again, Molly punched her pillow. Again, she tried to get it to lay just right under her long neck. But alas, it didn't work.

"Sheep," she said. "I hear some Mules count sheep to get to sleep."

So she counted. "One, two, three, four..." By two thousand and eighty-seven, she had given up hope.

"The ceiling," she thought, "I'll just look at the ceiling."

And so she did. For a very long time. For so long that her eyes began to hurt.

"It's dark, silly," she told herself. "You can't see anything."

"Close your eyes, Molly," she heard a kind voice say. "Close your eyes, dear, and go to sleep."

Hearing voices when there were none wasn't something Molly normally did. Okay, never did. At least not before this moment. But this one was so kind, so gentle, and it wasn't really like she

whisper in the privacy of the bathroom. A privacy rarely experienced.

"Yes, my darling. We have met. You've just forgotten. We've always known one another. I came to remind you. Let you know that you're never, never alone."

Her misty voice trailed off as the forceful knock on the door jarred Molly out of her reverie. "Molly! Out. Now!" her mother shouted. Her sing-song tone of voice from just a few minutes before had left. Gone away. And instead, another voice sternly commanded, "Time. To. Go!"

"Coming," Molly cried as she opened the door and quickly dashed to her room. "I was just spending time with Grandma Rose!" she explained while dressing.

"Grandma Rose!" her mother exclaimed. "You're such a silly Goose. She's been dead for years. Why, long before you were born."

Molly started to explain but stopped after blurting out a short, "I know, but..."

Let's get some food in you before your brain shuts down completely," her mother said.

Heading towards the kitchen, she called, "Jack, can you grab a piece of cheese toast for Molly?"

She then pulled Molly down the hall and pushed her out the door. "You'll have to eat in the car. I am not about to miss getting a seat up front for Christmas carols. Always, always, always my favorite."

Molly's
Grandmother
or
A Baptism

"Your mother always picks the most inopportune time to visit!" said Sarah while pouring Jack's coffee.

"I'm none too excited about her coming either! All that blasted talk about how we should be doing this, not that. How awful our Mule children are. Why when she was..."

"Stop!" Sarah said with such force she surprised even herself. "Jack, please stop. I know what we're going to hear when she's here, there's no need for a preview. Here's your coffee. And please, try not to spill it all over the floor."

"I don't spill it," said Jack as a large splash landed on the wood floor.

Saying nothing, Sarah simply gave Jack a sad look of 'I told you so.'

Completely oblivious, he left the room without a backward glance. Math papers were calling. It was grading time before the semester break.

Turning back to the food she had laid out, Sarah slowly, methodically began to prepare their evening meal. "Roast beef, mashed potatoes, green beans. Perfect. A protein, carbohydrate and green. Surely she can't complain about this meal not being balanced," said Sarah out-loud to no one in particular. No, that's not true. She was saying it to herself. Cheering herself up for what was to surely be a miserable week. Thank goodness she wasn't staying for Christmas. Thanks be to God for that little bit of grace.

"Mom!" called Molly, dashing into the kitchen with her plastic tray of leftovers. An apple core, an orange peeling, and lots and lots of cracker crumbs. "When's Grandmother coming?"

"She said she'd be here around 5:00. She knows we eat at 5:30, so I imagine she'll be hungry," her mother replied.

"Are you sure I can't sleepover at Harriet's tonight? They're watching the latest sci-fi show, and I hate to miss it," Molly begged.

"No, you may not. I realize you're not excited about her coming," and under her breath, "'No one is,' but she *is* your grandmother, and your father's mother deserves to be treated with respect."

"Even though she doesn't treat anyone else with respect?" asked Molly.

"Precisely, as far as knowing how to behave, just watch her and do the opposite. That'll always serve you well," her mother said.

"Sure," said Molly, not listening and already planning her day. "I'll be back!" she called as she rushed out the door.

"Be sure and be back well before 5:00. I'll have to wash around your ears before she gets here. And don't forget to leave all your muddy clothes outside!" her mother called, dreading the usual mess Molly made after a day of play, but also happy to have her out of the house.

"Okay," she said to herself, "that's all set. Now, to make sure her bedroom is ready."

The day passed quickly, and soon they all heard the doorbell,

"Ding-dong!"

"Alright everyone!" called Sarah to the rest of the family who were hiding downstairs. "Put on your best behavior! She's here. Time to come up."

"Ah, do we have to?" asked Marvin, still seated at the chess table where they had been playing.

"Yes, we all do," their father said, shoving Minnie and Molly up the stairs with Marvin bringing up the rear.

Jack's mother was already standing in the kitchen with Sarah. She wore a cardigan sweater buttoned only at the top and reading glasses, which hung around her neck. Her invisible white gloves were caressing each surface, looking for any place where she could find fault. She had never forgiven Jack for marrying a Horse Mare. Their long line of respectable Donkeyhood ended with, as she called it, that one careless act.

"Mother!" cried Jack. "Great to see you!" he lied.

"Well, it's certainly been a long time since you invited me," she said with a huff.

"Oh, Mother, you know you're welcome anytime," again he lied, thankful that the drive was so far and her commitments so constant.

"Hmmpf," she replied. "Well, aren't you going to show me to my room? It's been a long day, and I need to wash up."

Kicking Molly with his hind leg, Jack cued his youngest to do her duty. "Right this way, Grandmother," said Molly, giving Minnie a scathing look. She had lost the coin-flip. Loser had to play this part in their happy-family act.

"Is this your room, Molly?" asked her grandmother.

"Yes, mine and Minnie's," a statement she repeated each time her grandmother visited.

"And who likes the purple?" her grandmother asked.

"Minnie," she replied, again for the umpteenth time.

"I'll be right there," her grandmother said, clearly dismissing Molly.

Happy to be relieved, she rushed to the kitchen. "How long is she staying?" she asked her mother.

"A week," she replied, "And don't ask me again if you want to be able to sit down comfortably," she warned.

Before the rest of the family could enjoy that brief solitude, Grandmother returned. Gazing at the stovetop, she asked, "Roast beef?" staring at the meat creation on the platter.

"Yes," Sarah said, biting her tongue to keep from spitting out, "Can't you see? It's right in front of you. What'd you think it was? Roasted Donkey?"

"My favorite," Grandmother simply replied.

"I know," Sarah didn't say, "that's why I made it."

"Children!" she called out. "Time for grace. Places everyone!"

Sarah had strategically placed her mother-in-law next to Molly who was known for spilling her milk. At every meal. Yes, every meal. Rather than take the standard blame for being the cause of this infraction, Sarah deliberately sat across from Molly. Let her mother-in-law see for herself how this regular occurrence is an act of nature, an unstoppable force of Molly-ness.

"Mother," asked Jack, "will you do the honors of saying grace?"

"Certainly," she said. Grandmother considered herself to be the finest Christian on the planet. She made a point of showing everyone. All the time.

"Amen," she said, after reciting the entire chapter of Matthew, it seemed to Molly. The potatoes were cold. The carrots too, but before any of their off-spring could voice a complaint, both parents bore the look of 'don't-you-dare' into each one of them.

"Yum, Mom," said Molly, enjoying her first bite with gusto.

"Yeah," added Marvin. "Really great, Maw."

"Thanks," smiled their mother, glad to be appreciated.

"It's a little dry, if you ask me," added Grandmother.

"I didn't ask you," said Sarah silently to herself, grimacing instead. "Only one week, six more days," she told herself.

"So, Minnie," asked their grandmother, "how's school going for you?"

"Great," Minnie replied. "I got chosen to be in the school play."

Ignoring her granddaughter and turning to her son instead, she asked, "You allow this Jack? You allow them to be in theater?"

"Mother, it's a harmless play. It's a school project. It doesn't mean she'll become a professional actress."

"Well," she humpfed, "I certainly hope not. Those fools are the cause of our nation's moral downfall."

Crushed, Minnie swallowed herself up into a ball, deep in her gut. "I'd love to be an actress," she thought, not daring to vocalize her secret dream.

"And you Marvin?" she asked, turning to her only grandson, the middle Mule.

Careful to not share what he was really excited about, being chosen to be first-string on the school's football team, Marvin cautiously said, "I got an A on my math test last week."

"Oh," she gushed, "I'm so proud of you. Even though you're a Mule, you're showing some promise." Turning to her son she added, "He must get those skills from you. We've always been known for our sharp minds."

Marvin smiled at Minnie, silently saying, "See, I know how to play her. Just tell her what she wants to hear."

Minnie glared at her brother. Chewing and chewing on her mouthful of food, she willed this dinner to be over. She couldn't wait to get back to the play and memorizing her lines.

Molly knew what was coming, and before she could take another bite, her grandmother asked, "And you, how are things with you?" The absence of her name was felt by everyone. Everyone except their grandmother.

Molly quickly ran down the short list of her life: school, play, church. "What on it is safe?" she wondered.

"I got a new Bible for Bible drill," she said.

"You didn't have one already?" her grandmother snapped.

"Well, sure, I had the one that Minnie and then Marvin used, but I got my own. A brand new one," a gleam of pleasure sneaking out without her permission, despite her disappointment at that first practice.

"Humpf," she snorted. "Seems like you could have continued using what you had. I tell you," she said to no one in particular. She had risen so high on her soapbox that Molly could practically see the clouds surrounding her head. "The world today is going to hell in a handbasket. Hell in a handbasket, I tell you. Everyone needs to be like me," she added. "Frugal, practical, and very, very Christian."

"Yes, Grandmother," said Molly, two words she had found to be the best fallback. "Yes Grandmother" whether she agreed or not. Molly was quickly learning to not think for herself. To be a good girl. Nose to the grindstone and never, ever contradict your elders.

And as she bowed her head to her grandmother, her large head bumped her glass of milk. Molly gasped. She tried to catch it, but in a flash, it tipped. The milk poured onto her grandmother's lap. Baptizing her with Molly's infraction. With Molly's impetuous nature, which she found she could not control no matter how hard she tried.

No Pain, No Gain
or
Do You Hear What I Hear?

"Molly, all your math answers are wrong!" exclaimed Miss Granger.

"They can't be. I know I got them right!"

"Well, you didn't. You're not as smart as you think, Miss Molly Mule smarty-pants. Minnie and Marvin never gave me the trouble you're always giving me."

"I'm not giving you trouble..." said Molly.

"Miss Granger," said her Pig of a teacher.

"I'm not giving you trouble, Miss Granger. I did get them all right. I *know* I did."

"Betsy, will you please check them?" asked the teacher sweetly.

"Great, Betsy, the cutest Bunny on the planet, teacher's pet, is going to check my math," said Molly under her breath. Sure to be quiet enough to not catch her teacher's pink ears.

"She's right, Miss Granger," said Betsy. "They're all right."

"What?" gasped Miss Granger, grabbing Molly's paper from Betsy's paw.

This time, she actually looked at the calculations. Not just the answers on her cue sheet. And the answers were right. It was the calculations that were wrong.

Miss Granger's entire body began to shake. She became even

more pink. Her spots got bigger. Darker even. She looked like she was about to explode. Smoke was coming out of her snout and her curly tail was spinning so quickly that later on the playground the class laughed about how she'd gotten lift-off. Not much of a lift-off because 500 pounds is still 500 pounds. But at least a boar's hair of height had been visible under her hooves in that split second of pure rage.

"How could Molly be right?!? How dare she!" Miss Granger spit and sputtered.

But she was.

"Miss Granger," said Betsy timidly with a force that belied her size, "It looks like Molly just wrote the equations down wrong. When you said 11 times 2, she wrote 11 times 10. A much more difficult equation, if you ask me."

"Didn't ask you," she huffed.

"And she even got it right!" added Betsy, stretching her bunny body as tall as she could in order to see over Miss Granger's enormous back. "See? She wrote the right answer: one hundred and ten. That's a lot harder to get than 22."

Furious, angry, and humiliated to be caught making a mistake, Miss Granger quickly changed the subject.

"That's all the math for today, students. It's time for you to go outside. Except you, Molly Mule, you're staying inside."

But Molly had already left. She hadn't heard Miss Granger's last command just like she hadn't correctly heard the math equations.

Fortunately for her, her new BFF Betsy told Principal Smith what happened. Otherwise, Molly would have had the beating of her life.

"Thanks, Betsy," Molly told her later, relief washing over her like a cool mountain spring. "I'm sorry for all the things I've thought about you."

"Like what?" Betsy asked, afraid to hear but also dying to know.

"Like being a know-it-all teacher's pet. I'm sorry," she told her new friend. "Now I know what you're really like. It takes a lot of courage to stand up to Miss Granger. I'll never forget it."

And she never did.

"Molly," said Doctor Gruff just a few days later, "sit still! I need you to not move." He was trying to place a tuning fork on her forehead.

"It tickles," Molly laughed, shaking her head from side to side.

"Sarah, can you do anything?" asked the doctor. He gave her such a pleading look that it reminded Molly's mother of when she was about to give birth. "For such a gifted doctor," she thought, "he really is too shy for this line of work."

"Molly, do hold still," said her mother. "Remember that chocolate ice cream I promised if you were a good little Mule?"

"Yes," said Molly, suddenly able to restrain herself.

Chocolate ice cream has been known to work miracles. Make problems go away. A pint. A quart. A gallon. The size doesn't matter. Even a spoonful has been known to work its magic. Make everything better. "If only it'd help Molly hear," thought her mother, continuing to give Molly her "behave-or-else" look. "I've got to stay on top of her. That's what mothers do."

"Twaaaaang," went the tuning fork.

"Now, Molly," Doctor Gruff said, "I need you to focus. Which ear can best hear the turning fork?" he asked, moving the tuning fork from her forehead to behind her ear. "Please, Molly, concentrate."

She was concentrating so hard that she felt her eyes cross and practically go inside her skull. "Was it left?" she wondered. "Or right? And which is left? I keep forgetting."

"Doctor Gruff?" Molly asked, "which is my left?" "This one, Molly," he said, gently tapping her shoulder. "Then it's that one," she said with confidence.

Looking over at her mother, the doctor solemnly said, "That's what I thought. Molly has conductive hearing loss."

Her mother gasped, "Is it catching?"

"No, no," he said assuring her. "Molly cannot infect anyone. It's genetic."

"Genetic?" she asked.

"Yes, it mostly shows up every other generation. But there's no need to worry, Sarah," he added. "It's treatable. She'll respond to surgery."

"Oh!" Molly's mother gasped with relief. "It's treatable!" she cheered.

Molly watched this exchange between her mother and the doctor as if she were watching a ping pong match. Eyes on the doctor. Then on her mother. Back and forth they went until her neck began to get as tired as her ears.

"Molly, dear," her mother asked, "do you understand? It's treatable."

Seeing her daughter's confusion, she asked, "Do you even hear me? Do you understand what I'm saying?"

"Yes, Mom, it's treatable."

"Great," thought her mother. "She's not as far gone as I thought."

"What's treatable?" asked Molly.

"Why your ears, silly."

"No, Mom, I mean, what's that mean? Treatable? Does it have something to do with Halloween?" Molly's favorite holiday was Halloween. She loved dressing up and yelling at the top of her voice, "Trick or treat!?!" She was never quite sure if she was supposed to ask a question or make a demand.

"Oh," her mother laughed, happy that her daughter could hear her. Especially when being so close. "It means that it can be fixed. Cured. Healed. Made better."

"Oh," said Molly nonchalant. "Cool. I thought it meant you had to cut me open or something."

"Oh, well," said her mother, turning now to the doctor. She silently mouthed, "You did say surgery? Do you have to cut her open?"

"Nah, nah, no need to get your britches in an up-roar," he laughed. "It's a simple case of peeling back her ear drum, snapping the little stapes, that's the main problem," he explained, pointing to the bones of the middle ear in a large, synthetic model. "After breaking off part of the stapes, I'll tuck in a piece of titanium. One end goes in her footplate and the other end attaches to the stub." Turning to Molly he said, "And then you'll be as right as rain.

Hearing as well as those," he coughed, "rather large ears will allow."

Relieved that the doctor wouldn't be cutting her daughter open, she wanted to make sure Molly understood, "You'll just have to come back one day, lay down on the table, and you'll be as right as rain."

"I heard what he said Mom," said Molly. "There won't be any pain."

"Well," her mother said looking at Doctor Gruff for assistance, but he just began describing the process in more detail, "Molly, there will be a sedative, an injection, and then we'll need to ..."

"Get more ice cream!" her mother added in a flourish, doing her best to shut Doctor Gruff down before he could say anything to scare Molly. She knew that she was going to have a dickens of a time just getting Molly to return, much less accept an injection without kicking a fit, throwing up dust, or generally just being like her father.

"Ice cream!" cried Molly. "I scream, you scream, we all scream for ice cream."

"That's right, dear. Just go on outside, and I'll be right there. Ask the receptionist for a lollipop; I'm sure she'll be glad to give you one."

Molly didn't need any further coaxing. Out she went giving her mother a chance to talk to the doctor in private before his next patient.

"Is this really treatable?" she asked.

"Yes, it's really quite common. But she will need to lay low for a bit after the surgery. Give her ear time to heal. That titanium piece has really got to take hold for it to last."

"Hmm," Molly's mother thought, "that might not be so easy..."

But before she could give this any further thought, Nurse Barbara came running in. "Hurry doctor! We've got an emergency. A baby Mouse has gotten stuck in the mouth of a Goat!" she said frantically. "The boy's mother assures us it was an accident, but I'm not so sure." Casting an eye towards the waiting room she called severely, "Billy! Sit back down! And do *not* close your mouth! You won't be able to breathe if you do!" she lied.

Molly and her mother quickly slipped out of the doctor's office before either her classmate Billy or his mother could recognize them.

The ear surgery took place only a few weeks later.

"Do hold still, Molly," said Nurse Florence. "You do not want to make Doctor Gruff angry!"

"I'm trying to hold still," said Molly. Her teeth were chattering so loudly that it sounded like a collection of tin drums.

"You're cold, aren't you?" the nurse asked.

"Well, just a little," said Molly, shivering so strongly that her thin blanket kept falling off.

"Oh, dear," the nurse said. "We have to keep everything cold for sanitation purposes, but maybe another blanket won't hurt anything."

"Thank you," Molly chattered. Not only was the stainless-steel table cold, it was slippery. Molly was doing her darndest not to slide off.

"Here you go," said the nurse as she carefully wrapped another blanket around Molly. "I pulled a fresh one out of the warmer. Now be sure and tuck your baby doll under the blanket," she added.

"Okay," said Molly, thankful that they let her bring her stuffed toy with her.

"I recommend that you look the other way," the nurse said as she pulled out a hypodermic needle.

"Why?" asked Molly. "Oh!" she gasped as she caught sight of the longest needle she had ever seen.

"There, there," said Nurse Florence gently, "It won't hurt too badly."

"Oh, what am I saying?" she asked herself, realizing that it would be best to tell this patient the truth. "Molly, my dear, it's going to hurt like heck. The more you can relax, the less it will hurt."

Molly's entire body clenched despite the nurse's instructions. She felt it go in. "Ouch!" she cried.

"Try to relax," the nurse repeated.

"Relax, Molly," she told herself. "Oh," herself replied, "it hurts. It really, really hurts!"

"It's the anesthesia going in, dear, that hurts," said the nurse trying to comfort her. "Just a few more minutes."

"Minutes?" asked Molly through clinched teeth. Tears were rolling down her face from the pain.

"Almost done," said the nurse, glancing at the large clock on the wall. "There, one minute's passed. The next will be over before you know it."

"I don't really need to hear," Molly impulsively told the nurse. "Maybe you can just stop."

"Oh, don't be silly," said the nurse. "Everyone needs to be able to hear."

"What about the deaf?" asked Molly. "They need to hear, but they can't because they're deaf."

"Now, now, Molly, dear," said the nurse, "don't worry about silly things. Try to relax. We're the adults here; we'll take care of you." "That's right," said Dr. Gruff as he burst into the room, "Leave everything to me." Turning to Nurse Florence he asked, "Is she ready to go?"

"Just about," the nurse replied. "Molly! Molly!" she called into her patient's good ear. "You're going to get sleepy, but you won't fall asleep completely. You'll still be able to follow what's happening. Okay?"

"Okay," Molly yawned.

"That's my girl," said Doctor Gruff. "You'll be hearing out of your right ear in no time."

Not long after, two Goat orderlies came in to assist. "Right this way boys," said Doctor Gruff, directing them to the side door. "Molly!" he shouted, "We're going into the operating room now."

"Okay," she tried to reply, but a glob of saliva came out instead.

"You can clean that up later," said Doctor Gruff to Nurse Florence. "Just keep her moving. Keep her moving."

Once Molly's gurney was set in the operating room, Doctor Gruff began. "Nice job, Nurse Florence," he said looking over the trays of supplies. "Good work."

"Thanks," Nurse Florence blushed. Compliments from the

doctor were rare indeed.

"Molly," said the doctor, again speaking as if into a megaphone. "We're going to start the surgery soon. You won't feel a thing, but you will be able to hear us. Out of your left ear, that is. But now, this is important. I'm going to tilt the table so that I can better access your ear. We're also going to wrap some more blankets around you to hold you in place."

Hospital orderlies quickly began wrapping Molly up like a mummy. Panic began to fill her every pore. "Do you have to?" she asked frantically. "Does it have to be so tight?"

"Feeling a little claustrophobic, are we?" asked Doctor Gruff.

"I don't know about you," Molly drooled. "But, yes sir. I am. Can't I just hold on?"

"Well," he pondered, "I suppose that could work." Speaking to the orderlies, he said, "You can just wrap them around her to catch the blood."

"Blood?" asked Molly. Beep. Beep. Beep. Beep. Beep. Beep. Her heart monitor began to beep furiously.

"Not much, Molly," the doctor said, trying to reassure her, "not much at all. For a Mule, that is. We Goats would have less, but still, Molly, not all that much."

Feeling very unassured, Molly realized that she was about to slide off the table. She quickly slid her right legs around the table and held on for dear life. "I can't let them notice," she thought. "I can't let them wrap me up like a mummy."

"Doing alright, Molly?" the doctor asked.

"Yes," Molly lied. "Calm down, Molly," she told herself. "You're as strong as an Ox. You can hold on. I know you can." Gradually, the panic receded. Molly felt herself relax. A little. Until she felt some kind of liquid cold slide into her right ear. And in that moment, she fainted. Or fell asleep. She never knew. Fortunately, she had hooked herself so securely onto the table that she didn't fall off.

Molly started to come to just as Doctor Gruff said to Nurse Florence, "That's a mighty fine job I did, if I say so myself. That extra-large titanium piece did the trick. Settled into her footplate nicely. And," he said winking at Nurse Florence, "It helps that Mules' stapes are about the size of my leg."

Turning toward his patient, he shouted, "Molly! Can you hear me?"

It felt as if he had poked a sharp needle straight into Molly's right ear. The pain slid down to her spine, hips, legs. Her entire body shook. "Yes," she whispered, gasping for breath.

"Great!" he shouted back not noticing Molly's discomfort.

"Doctor," said Nurse Florence forcefully, "don't you see that she's in pain. She can hear out of that ear now. There's no need to shout."

"Oh," he chuckled, "so she can." But not changing his tone, he said to Molly, "See, just leave everything to me."

You Can't Always Have Fun
or
Can You?

"You can't always have fun!" shouted Miss Granger from the other side of the classroom. Molly's few weeks of rest after the surgery had passed. Healed, her ear had no trouble understanding her teacher.

"See?" said Billy. "I told you so."

Molly chose to ignore him *and* her teacher. Picking up all the balloons she had just dropped, she started blowing them up again. Molly was decorating the room for her new best friend's birthday party.

Stretch. Pucker. Blow. Stretch. Pucker. Blow. Over and over again until she had inflated the entire case. "That's 12 times 12. Wow!" she said, forgetting herself and speaking out loud. "One hundred and forty-four balloons!"

"And that's 144 too many," said Miss Granger, taking a pin to them one-by-one.

"Pop. Pop. Pop."

"But ..." said Molly, "you said I could throw a party for Betsy."

"Yes, but I didn't say you could crowd the entire room with balloons. What a mess," her teacher said as she systematically popped each balloon. One-by-one, "Pop. Pop. Pop," until there was a dead pile of rubber all over the floor. "Now clean up that mess!"

she shouted. "Betsy, dear," she then said apologetically, "I'm sorry for this mess. Let me throw you a good party. Not with blown up balloons but with helium-filled ones. Won't that be fun?" she asked with a smile.

"Yes," said Betsy, feeling a little guilty but excited all the same. "I'm sorry," she said to Molly with her eyes. "It's okay," Molly replied silently as she continued to pick up the shattered balloons.

"So why'd you let me blow them up if you were just going to pop them?" asked Molly in a rare combination of defiance and bravery.

"So I could have the pleasure of seeing you clean them up," her teacher replied demonically. She did not like Molly the Mule, and everyone knew it. Most of all, Molly.

"Class dismissed," she called about five minutes before the bell. "But not for you missy," she said to Molly. "Once you're finished, I'd like you to sweep and mop the floor. And get the helium bottle out from the closet. The rest of the class will fill up the balloons after lunch. Surely, you've had your fill of balloons," she laughed.

Molly simply stood still. Limp. Wondering what she had done to make her teacher hate her so much.

"Okay class," said Miss Granger, "time to clean up!"

It had been a rare day in Miss Granger's class. She had decided to give them a bit of fun. That is, everyone except Molly who she had sent Molly to the principal's office to explain why she wasn't included.

"Hmm," said Principal Smith when Molly entered his office. "It hasn't been that long since your last visit. What happened this time?"

"I'm not really sure," answered Molly. "Miss Granger said we were going to do an art project. But then she said not me. And I'm not really sure why. She just doesn't seem to like me, sir. She's always comparing me to Minnie and Marvin and saying that they got all the brains."

"Well, that happens sometimes," the principal replied.

"That siblings get all the brains?" asked Molly with shock.

"No, no," he laughed. "That a teacher just doesn't like a student. Most of the time, there's a real good reason," he said, reflecting on past cases. "The student doesn't listen. Breaks things. Is a royal pain in the neck, but...well, Molly," he said, taking a moment to choose his words wisely, "I think in your instance, it has nothing to do with you. Nothing at all."

"Then why?" asked Molly.

"Oh, that's a really long story," he said. "And I think your mother could shed light on it."

"My mother?"

"Yes, well, you see, Sarah, your mother, and Elvira, Miss Granger," he explained after seeing the confusion on Molly's face, "they were classmates at the orphanage."

"Oh," said Molly, careful to stay quiet and just listen. Her mother rarely shared stories from her past, and Molly didn't want to jeopardize this unusual opportunity to learn something new about her mother by interrupting the principal.

"Well, I don't know a lot," he said. "And, well, Molly, it's not really my place to tell these stories. Surely your mother's explained..." But from the look on Molly's face, he saw that she hadn't.

"Hmm," he said, "I'm not surprised. I imagine it would have been difficult for her."

He waited for a moment and continued. "Embarrassing really. A Horse of her stature having to live with, with Pigs, Goats, all kinds of other animals from all types of backgrounds."

"Oh," said Molly again, "I'd never thought of it that way."

She took a moment to ponder Principal Smith's muscular Quarter Horse build. "A most beautiful red," she thought. "And I love his white socks." Blushing in spite of herself, she realized that he and her mother were similar types. At least on the outside. In physical appearance.

"Well," he coughed, bringing Molly out of her reverie, "I think you're getting the point. Sometimes, it's not about us. Well, actually, it never really is. So, Molly, dear, just do your best to stay out of her way. Miss Granger has an ax to grind, but it's not with you."

"Okay," said Molly tentatively. "But then why does she like Minnie and Marvin so much? But not me?"

"Molly, you won't believe it, but I can remember having similar conversations with your siblings. Adults sometimes forget. Selective memory loss we call it. I'd say this is one of those instances."

"Yes," thought Molly. "Grown-ups are tricky. They say one thing, but do another. Act like they want to listen, but then say you're talking too much. The Crossleys though are different."

Sighing, Molly decided to take a risk by sharing with Principal Smith what was really troubling her. "Well," she said, stepping into the unknown, "she tells me over and over that I can't always have fun. That I have to work hard. Study. Do my homework. Well, I know that. I know we have to do all that stuff. But, but can't we still have fun while we're doing it? I mean, what's the point of living if it's all work and no play?"

Principal Smith smiled. There were parts of his job he loved, and this was one of them. "Molly," he said, "I want you to know that I hear you, and you're right. Society and teachers will tell you that you can't always have fun."

"What?" asked Molly, certain that she had just done the dumbest thing yet in her short life, speaking honestly to a school principal.

"Hear me out," he said, seeing her panic. "I'll explain. No," he said, giving it a second thought, "I'll show. We've got time before your lunch period. Let's take a little walk."

And what happened next would stay in Molly's memory forever. Long after her school lunches, dances, and even grades had fallen to the wayside, Molly would remember this one and only walk with Principal Smith down to his workshop.

Once they reached the back of the school, he unlocked two large double-doors to an outbuilding. "It's okay, Molly," he said. "Go on in and have a look around. I'll just wait right here."

Despite the wide beam of light shining through the open doors, it was still very dark in the windowless workshop. Molly tripped over a collection of tin cans, scaring herself half to death. "Are you alright?" he called. "Yes," she simply replied.

"Good," he said laughing, relieved that she hadn't injured herself. "The light's on the right. And don't worry," he added, "you can't break a thing."

"Click." Molly easily found the switch. She waited a bit for her eyes to adjust, and then slowly objects began to take shape. A fire pit. Cold. Full of ash. Clearly it had been used innumerable times. Metal. Lots and lots of metal in various shapes and sizes. Her mother's voice came to her in the form of a memory, "Principal Smith moonlights as a blacksmith," she heard her say. "That's right," thought Molly. "I'd forgotten."

"What do you think?" he asked from his post outside.

"It's nice," said Molly, not sure what to say and wondering why he'd brought her here.

"Why did I bring you here?" he asked.

Yes, she silently nodded, surprised that an adult had read her mind so easily.

"Most everybody sees this place simply as a place to work."

"Duh," her face said.

"To do messy, physical work," he added. "But to me. To me, it's sacred."

"Huh?" asked Molly.

"Yes," he laughed. "To me this is heaven on earth."

"Okay," said Molly, not understanding.

"This is a place," he continued, "where I can truly be myself. Not have to worry about students. Whether they're safe or being well cared for. Here I can just bang on metal and mold to my heart's content."

"Okay," she said again.

"But," he said with excitement, "I can also have fun. A blast, in fact."

Molly was slowly seeing the light.

"So, yes, Molly," he said. "You do have to work. Study. Do your homework. All that. But...I'm here to tell you that you can still have fun. No matter *what* you're doing."

"Wow," thought Molly, rendered speechless.

"But," he sadly added, "I'm one of the few who feel this way. In our society it's more important to complain. To tell each other how hard our job is. How little free time we have. We make a contest out of it, and whoever has the worst life wins. But," he said, taking a pause, "if you find that you can enjoy yourself, Molly, no matter what you're doing, no matter what you're experiencing, you'll live a much more peace filled life. That's for sure."

They were both silent for several minutes. Heads bowed in awe at the power of what Principal Smith had just said. Then, raising his head with a hopeful smile, he added, "And maybe, just maybe the rest of the world will catch up one day to this simple truth."

"Sorry you had to miss it," said Betsy when Molly met her in the lunch room a few minutes later. "It was actually fun."

"It's okay," said Molly, not at all sorry that she had been sent to the principal's office. "Really, it's fine."

And it was.

She never told anyone about that visit. About what she had experienced. "And why should I?" she thought. "That was for me.

And me alone."

I Don't Want
to Go to
Hell
or
Do I Have To?

"I don't want to go to hell," Molly thought to herself. She laid in bed listening to the rustling of the trees outside while doing her best to not touch Minnie who laid beside her.

"I do not want to go to hell," she thought again.

This solitary discussion had been repeating itself almost non-stop since her last Sunday school class. Mrs. Hare wanted them all to know what would happen if they didn't invite Jesus into their hearts.

"Was she trying to scare us?" Molly wondered.

"No, I'm trying to save you from eternal damnation!" Molly imagined her saying. "Leave me alone!" Molly silently screamed. But the image of smoke and flames rose higher and higher, haunting Molly throughout the night. She tossed and turned and completely forgot about how she had felt when in Grandma Rose's presence. That night she'd been comforted, that night she had slept, but this night she only felt terror.

"Didn't sleep well?" asked her mother the next day as Molly's head practically fell into her cheese toast. Molly nodded herself back upright and mumbled, "No."

But she didn't want to talk about it. Especially not with her mother. She also didn't want to be there. She wished she could disappear into the sleep that had never come.

"Worried about something, dear? A test? Is that Billy Goat giving you a hard time again?" her mother persisted.

"No, everything's fine," said Molly with as much enthusiasm as a Snail going to a French restaurant. "Peachy keen."

"Well, that's great," her mother replied. "Time to get going. You don't want to miss the bus. I've got decorators coming, and I can't keep them waiting. Out the door, missy" she said, pulling Molly up out of the chair and shoving her out the door. "Have a great day!" she called as Molly ran towards the bus which had just arrived. "See you this afternoon!"

Later at school, Molly finished her math exercises before the rest of the class. She used the time to ponder this most delightful topic once again: "I don't want to go to hell."

"And why should I?" she thought. "I've never killed anyone. Though I have wanted to hurt Billy," she thought apologetically. "I share my toys. Well, usually. Why would God want to send me to hell? I don't get it."

"Molly!" Miss Granger screeched. "What in tarnation are you doing? Leave that globe alone!"

In the midst of her worrying, Molly had picked up the classroom globe and begun to twirl it on the tip of her hoof. Kind of like the Harlem Globetrotters. Molly's world was spinning off its axis. Africa, Brazil, Antarctica flew by. Imaginary folk were holding on with all their might. "Why do you want to send me to hell?" Molly asked God for the umpteenth time.

"Thwack!"

"Ouch!" cried Molly as the extra-large encyclopedia volume S landed on her head. Miss Granger had climbed up the sliding ladder and begun pulling thick volumes off the shelf. M for Molly's back. Q for her nose. And Z, Z she saved for last. "Perfect for her knees," thought Miss Granger. "Thwack, thwack, thwack," as she continued to whack Molly.

"Ouch!" said Molly repeatedly. "She's lucky I don't give her a good kick," she thought. Miss Granger's rearranging of encyclopedias succeeded in pulling Molly out of her fog of doom and gloom and

eternal damnation. Real, present physical pain had pushed her imagined terror aside for the moment.

"Get back to your desks!" Miss Granger yelled. For by now the entire classroom was in an uproar. All the students had left their desks. Everyone was afraid of Miss Granger's unpredictable aim.

"Get back to work!" she screamed.

"I'm done. I already did my work," said Molly.

"You have, have you? Let me be the judge of that," she huffed, gruffly taking Molly's papers from her desk.

"Class, get back to work. And since Miss Molly here seems to think she's in charge of things, I've added another assignment to your list. Make a list of all the countries you can remember which are on the globe that Molly practically destroyed."

"Awww, not more work," moaned Billy, shooting invisible daggers at Molly.

"Phuuu," Molly replied while sticking out her tongue.

"It's okay," said Betsy. "I love thinking about all the countries in the world. All the places I want to travel to!" she exclaimed.

"Yeah, right. Like Bunnies can travel," Billy muttered.

"Of course, we can," she shouted. "Haven't you ever heard of the Playboy Bunnies? They get around."

"They sure do," said Billy with a wicked grin. "Sure, you can, Betsy," countered Molly.

Turning her focus once again towards Billy, Molly did her best to shoot him a grimace which rivaled that of all the poor souls stuck in hell.

"Class! For the last time. Back to work! And Molly, I want you to stay after and help me clean up," shouted their teacher.

"Yes, Miss Granger," said Molly dejectedly. She hadn't wanted to get the rest of the class in trouble. She never did.

"Ring, ring, ring." With the sounding of the bell, the class hurriedly put their assignments away, tucking them deep into their desks. Miss Granger liked a tidy room, and they all knew the consequences of not following her rules. Just look at Molly, who already had the mop and bucket in tow.

"I'm a clean Pig," she often told the class, determined to never be compared to others of her kind who lived out in the country.

"You missed a spot," Miss Granger yelled. Surveying the floor with her magnifying glass, Miss Granger was a Sow Sherlock Holmes. All that was missing was her Watson. Unless Betsy, the class pet, fulfilled that role. "Funny," Molly thought as she navigated the mop between rows and rows of desks, "she never has to clean. In fact," she mused, "no one else ever does. Except Billy, and somehow he doesn't count."

This mindless work gave Molly time once again to think, ponder, and stew: "I don't want to go to hell!" She became so worked up that she accidentally splattered water all over the floor. "Molly! What am I going to do with you? Clean up that mess. I've got to go to the library," her teacher announced, as if the pope himself were there to receive her. "When you're finished, meet me there."

"Yes, Miss Granger," Molly said. "I'll be there as soon as I'm done."

"Finished!" Miss Granger corrected. "Not done. I would have to stick a fork in your hind parts to see if you were done."

"Yes, Miss Granger," Molly sighed. "As soon as I'm finished."

"Wow, that was lucky," thought Molly as she continued to maneuver the mop. "I thought she'd never leave." Even though Miss Granger removed herself from the room, Molly's worries remained, to go (to hell) or not to go. That is the question.

By the time Molly finished and put the mop and bucket back in their designated spots, recess was over. The rest of the class returned and went straight to their seats. No one liked to be caught off guard by their teacher.

"Miss Molly!" her teacher shouted as she entered the room. "I thought I asked you to come to the library when you finished."

"I just did. I mean, I just finished."

Looking around the room, Miss Granger reviewed its cleanliness. Floor clean. Check. Dry. Check. Mop put away. Check. "So, you have," she nodded with reluctant approval. "So, you have." Addressing the entire class, she said, "It's time now for science."

They all groaned. Everyone hated science as taught by Miss Granger. Even those who loved science hated it. Using this subject as her personal soapbox, she preached that science was largely to blame for evil in the world. "It was a simpler time when I was young. Much simpler."

"This day is never going to end!" thought Molly as she pulled out her science book. And yet it did. Finally. Magically. A gust of wind blew through the slightly opened window and brought with it a freshness, unexpected but greatly appreciated.

"Ring!" The last bell of the day.

"Be sure to clean up your desks!" Miss Granger called out needlessly. She had put the fear of God in each and every student. Even those who never made their beds at home, tidied their desks for Miss Granger.

"And bring that report you've been working on," she continued. "Tomorrow everyone gets five minutes for their presentation."

Silent moans filled the class as they hurried toward the door. "I haven't even started," said Billy, ignored by his classmates who were used to his laziness.

Molly was the last to leave. Despite the way her teacher treated her, Molly still felt she should show respect. "Thank you, Miss Granger," she said, "for letting me clean the floor. It gave me some time to think."

"What an odd thing to say," Miss Granger thought as she quickly pushed Molly aside. Unsure of how to respond to Molly's gratitude, she simply turned her back to her student and began to focus on the following day.

Molly's bus ride home was pleasantly uneventful. Billy got picked up by a family member, so he wasn't there to harass her. Minnie had dance class, so she had walked straight there. And Marvin had gone to his daily football practice.

"Wow," thought Molly. "More time to think," quickly returning to the groove she was forming in her brain. "I don't want to go to hell. I don't want to go to hell. And why would Jesus want me to? The Jesus I know is sweet and kind. He visits me at night. Smiles at me. That sounds more like something Billy would want. Not Jesus."

Once off the bus, she slowly walked home. The day ended like all others. "Be sure and brush your teeth, Molly. And say your prayers." And still, she hadn't found an answer. "Why would God want to send anyone to hell?"

Molly to the Rescue
or
We Can Win With Five

"Great shot, Betsy!" cried Molly, secretly amazed that her tiny friend managed to hit the ball with the tip of her ear.

"Thanks," Betsy replied. "And thanks for being there to get it over the net. I love how you use all your hooves."

"That's what they're there for!" cried Molly with an enormous grin on her toothy face.

"Move over," shouted Billy as he shoved Betsy off the court. "We don't need you on our team. We can win with five players. That's how worthless you are!"

"Ohhhh," cried Betsy as she landed on her bunny belly on the other side of the gym, coming to a screeching halt loud enough to wake an Owl.

"Step back!" cried Molly, showing Billy her full height. "Step back or you'll be sorry!"

"Oh yeah, step back or what? Everybody knows you're a goody two shoes. Miss Molly the Mule," he sang mockingly, "never breaks a rule."

"I'm...giving you a chance," she stuttered. "Leave her alone. She's doing her best!"

"And her best ain't good enough. We don't need her to win!"

"It doesn't matter if we need her or not, she's on the team, so she stays!" said Molly forcefully. "Come on back, Betsy!" she called across the gym. "We need you!"

"Yeah, right," said Billy under his breath, suddenly aware that Miss Granger had returned.

"Keep it going students! Pfff. Pfff. Pfff," the teacher whistled. "Where's your ball, Billy?" she asked. "Looks like it's your turn to serve." And with that their teacher went to the other side of the gym.

"You got lucky, Molly," said Billy with a glare. "Saved by the Pig."

"Her name is Miss Granger."

"Yeah? So what. She's still a Pig."

"And you're a Goat," said Molly.

"And you're a Mule," he countered.

"Wow, you knock me over with your gift of observation. Serve already," she said, turning towards her tiny friend. "That's right Betsy. You're in the center front now. I've got you covered."

"Thwump." Billy served. The ball barely made it over. But over it went. One. Two. Three. The other side shot the ball back in perfect form.

"Great job, y'all!" cried Molly.

"Whose side are you on?" asked Billy as he breathlessly pushed Molly aside for a quick return, hogging the ball with a single hit, including no one else on his team. "You're not the entire school's cheerleader," he complained.

"And you're not the only player on this team," she countered, hurriedly getting back into position, back row center. Hooves up, ready to hit. She was just in time for the next ball, which came right to her. "Twack." Straight up. A perfect set. Easy for tiny Betsy to reach. But before she could get her tiny bunny paws on the ball, she was knocked clear across the gym. Again. Billy took a careless swipe at the ball, which did manage to cross the net but then hit the ground with a "Thunk." The other team was so mad that they too had taken their eyes off the ball.

Molly flew so swiftly to where Betsy lay that her classmates later called it magic. Crouching by her friend's side, she gently asked, "Are you alright, Betsy? Did he break anything?"

"Nah, I'm fine," she answered, barely hiding back her tears. "Let's just go back to the game. You don't need to make a fuss over me." Carefully picking herself up, Betsy slowly bounced back.

But instead of returning to the game, Molly felt a fury rise up within her. A fury so fierce that it felt like the righteousness of God. Turning her backside to Billy, she kicked with all her might. "Ooomp," he moaned. She'd made direct contact with Billy's gut.

"Bam." The opponents' ball landed in their court. Point lost.

"That's okay!" called Sally from the other side. "We'll give you the point. Play on."

"Thanks!" said Molly, getting back into position. "I think we can win this game with only five players," she said, cheering her teammates on.

Seeing that he wasn't wanted and shocked that Miss Granger hadn't come to his rescue, Billy crawled off the court. He never gave them that kind of grief again. Especially when Miss Molly was playing.

I Still Don't Want to Go to Hell
or
Will It Hurt?

"Hurry up Molly; we're waiting!" her mother called.

"Why do I have to wear these shoes?" Molly asked.

"Because good little Mules wear patent leather shoes."

"Why?"

"Because I said so," her mother replied.

"But I hate them. They hurt, and I don't like how shiny they are."

"You'll wear them. And you'll like them," her mother shouted, giving Molly the look that meant a belt was in the works if she didn't comply.

"Alright," Molly said, tugging on the shoes and doing her best to look pitiful and show how uncomfortable they were.

"Now march right out, little lady, or we'll be late to church."

Molly liked going to church. They served juice and crackers. Really tasty. But she didn't like it when they talked about hell. Told you how you would go there if you didn't believe. "Why would God want to send me to hell?" Molly wondered, still unable to put this to rest.

On this particular day at church there weren't any threats, but still, Molly knew that they lay just under the surface. Underneath all of the nice nice.

"Molly," Mrs. Hare asked, "where will your soul go when you die? Have you asked Jesus to come into your heart?"

Molly squirmed. She hadn't asked him yet because she just wasn't sure. Yes, she liked Jesus. Liked that he loved all the little children – red, and yellow, black and white – but she didn't feel right knowing that others would go to hell.

"How can he be so wonderful to some but not to all?" she wondered. "Just because they didn't invite him over for dinner.

Okay, it's into your heart, but it feels like the same thing," she thought while having another private conversation on the topic. "I want a Jesus who loves everybody. Not just some. And how can he fit into our hearts anyway?"

"Molly?" Mrs. Hare asked again, slowly bringing Molly back to earth. "Are you ready?"

"I'm not sure," she said. Molly struggled just to say that. She really wanted to be left alone.

"Don't worry dear, no one's going to force you," her teacher said.

"Yeah, right," felt Molly.

Turning her attention from Molly to Billy, Mrs. Hare continued, "Billy, I'm so proud of you. Asking Jesus into your heart. That took a lot of courage."

"He just wants to go swimming," Molly thought. "He can't really be sorry for all his sins. Not when he still takes everyone's crayons at school."

But she didn't dare say what she was thinking. Molly was too good of a little Mule to do that. She had learned her lessons well. Follow directions. Don't run with scissors. Always put the lid back on the glue. No, she wasn't about to say what she really thought. That just got you into trouble. And Molly didn't like trouble. She liked for everyone to get along. "If you make waves," she thought, "everyone just gets wet."

"Alright class," Mrs. Hare said, "time for juice and crackers."

Directing her attention again to Billy she asked, "Do you want me to walk down the aisle with you?" "Nah," he replied, "I can go by myself." "I'm so proud of you," she beamed.

Molly and the rest of the class rolled their eyes. Mrs. Hare didn't know the real Billy. Only the kids on the playground knew him.

But still. There was an awful feeling in Molly's gut. A yucky, awful feeling. She didn't want to go to hell when she died. "That would be terrible! Hot. Miserable. And would it hurt?" she wondered. "They say it lasts forever."

Even so, she couldn't quite gather the courage. And she definitely didn't want Mrs. Hare joining her. "Do you really have to walk down that aisle and get baptized to not spend the rest of eternity in hell?" she wondered.

"Maybe Billy's brave after all," she thought. "He doesn't seem to have any problem lying, so that he'll go to heaven rather than hell."

But Molly, she was too good. She couldn't lie. Not about this. It was much too serious.

Until...about six months later. She just couldn't stand it. The thought of dying and spending the rest of eternity in hell just ate at her.

"Okay," she told herself, "you just have to ask Jesus in. How much can that hurt? Besides, he already comes to visit all the time. How different will it be?"

So, she sat with it. And sat with it. A month of Sundays passed until almost all of her friends had walked down that aisle. Mrs. Hare didn't give her any grief. Molly still got to drink the juice, eat the crackers, play all the games, including going roller skating. But still, she wasn't part of the clique. The special group that got that knowing smile from Mrs. Hare.

"What would it be like to spend all eternity in hell?" she wondered. It's not like she could ask anyone. Everyone she knew had asked Jesus into their hearts.

"Well," she thought, "except Harriet and Harry. They hadn't. The Crossleys don't go to church. But surely Jesus wouldn't send them to hell. Surely not."

And then one day, the pressure built up so greatly that Molly just couldn't stand it. And without realizing what she was about to do, she stood up and walked down that aisle. All eyes turned and stared. "That's Molly," they whispered to one another, "Jack and Sarah's youngest."

"Molly," Father Bob gently asked, "are you ready to invite Jesus in? Accept him as your Lord and Savior? Ask him to forgive you for all your sins?"

"Yes," Molly lied. And if she'd had the courage to say what she was really feeling, it would have been, "I don't want to go to hell, Father Bob. I just don't want to go to hell."

The Middle Years:
Still Slightly Damp

Jack's Mother
or
Molly's Grandmother:
Take Two

"Yes, Mother," said Jack. "I know you don't have space for us anymore. Yes, I know it's the busy time of year."

He was talking on the phone with his mother, Molly's grandmother. An activity he savored as much as a tooth pulling. Every few seconds Jack rolled his eyes as his mother continued to bark orders.

"I can hear her all the way over here!" his wife said from the other side of the room where she was listening with all her might. "Shush!" mouthed Jack.

"But, but," he said forcefully, interrupting his mother, "Sarah and I have discussed it, and we want to find a place to stay when we're there. We'll wing it."

"You can't wing it!" his mother screamed. "Our family makes plans! We are *not* flighty like Birds!"

Her scream was so loud that Jack quickly moved the phone about a yard over his head. Returning it to his ear he said, "Yes, Mother, I do hear what you're saying, but it will just have to wait. I've got to get off the line. The egg timer is about..."

"Click." Three minutes had passed. All the sand had run from the top of the timer to the bottom. The operator had disconnected the call.

"Whew," he said, "was she ever spitting mad!"

"I see," said Sarah as she crossed the room and wiped a big glob of drool off the side of her husband's face.

"Madder than a hornet. Nothing would make her happier than seeing us all get arrested for camping illegally. Can you imagine? You, me, Minnie, Marvin, and Molly all locked up for camping without a permit," he laughed.

"But not before her grand reception," his wife said. "Think about it, dear, she wouldn't want us to miss that."

"No, she wouldn't," he agreed. "She needs us there to make her look good."

"Besides," added Sarah, "how else could she rub it in later if we weren't there to witness her most grand donation? The best feeding shed ever built!" Sarah said in a mocking broadcaster voice.

"And with a brass bell!" said Marvin entering the room, anxious to join in on the fun. "And some kind of fancy piping!" added Minnie not too far behind. Their parents fought so frequently that any moment of peace was savored and celebrated.

"What's going on?" asked Molly as she rushed into the room, frothing at the mouth. "Not in here, young Mare," her mother said, shooing her off. "Bathrooms are where you brush your teeth. Not kitchens."

"But what'd I miss?" she asked, doing her best to stay in the room. Like her siblings, Molly didn't like missing out on any fun.

"Nothing you need to worry your big 'ole head about. Now off with you and don't come back until you're finished," her mother scolded. "And while you're at it," she added, "clean your room!"

Her mother wasn't really angry. In fact, she was happy. Nothing gave her more pleasure than seeing her husband stand up to his mother. Her mother-in-law. Not that it happened very often. "Yes," she thought, "that's what makes this so especially delicious."

"Sarah," said Jack, "I don't think I've ever seen you any happier."

"Well," she said snuggling up to him and running her nose along his mane, "you sure told her. And about time! I'm so glad we can't camp at her new place. That last time was miserable. Don't you remember? She kept poking her head in, 'Isn't it about time you polished the trailer? Washed your dishes? And haven't you finished that silly card game yet?'" said Sarah, mocking her mother-in-law's shrill voice.

"Yeah," said Marvin, "we never did get to finish that game."

"I know," laughed Minnie, enjoying the fun. "'Cards are the devil's workshop!'" she said mockingly. "I didn't find my ace of spades until the next day when I took a bath," she laughed. "I had hid it in my pants!"

"That's why you Mares need to wear pockets," said Marvin.

"Yes," agreed their father, tapping his chest. "This shirt pocket has saved me a million times. All the things I've hid there over the years."

"And that pocket protector doesn't hurt either," laughed Minnie.

"Are y'all talking about Grandmother?" asked Molly as she returned to the room. Her mouth was no longer covered in foam. And she was even wearing her nicest pair of cutoffs.

"Who else, dear?" laughed their mother. "She's the one creature we can all have a good laugh over."

"Ahh," said Jack. "That's the nicest thing you've ever said about her."

"Well," she said unusually coy, "she did bring you into the world. And without you, I wouldn't have my Minnie, Marvin, or Molly."

"Ahh," said Molly, feeling a warmth from her head to her hooves.

"Thank you, Mother," said Jack to the now hung-up phone. "No one unites this family better than you."

Before they knew it, the time arrived for the entire family to pile in their family's station wagon and head to Florida.

"Jack, do stop," said Sarah. "I can't read the map while we're moving."

"I can," called Marvin from the rear of their station wagon.

"Brilliant idea, son. Pass it on back," he said to his wife.

After handing the crumpled map back to Minnie and Molly, who then passed it on to Marvin, their mother turned and straightened her blouse. "Well," she said, "we'll need to find a place soon. Your mother's apartment is close, I think."

"We'll find a place, don't you worry," said Jack with a smile as he faced the crowded Florida traffic.

"Hey Dad," called Marvin, "I see a place. It's called 'Bed, Bunk and Be Gone.'"

"We don't need beds, son, nor bunks," his father said. "We've got everything we need."

"I know," Marvin replied. "But it looks like it's got places for trailers too."

"Alright then," his father said, "we'll check it out. Where is it?"

"There!" shouted Marvin, pointing up ahead. "Just past that gas station!"

"Perfect," said Jack as he clicked on the right blinker and then easily changed lanes. "Perfect timing, son."

They were living *in the flow*. Long before anyone they knew used that expression. Rather than book a place in advance, they had simply trusted that they would find *what* they needed *when* they needed. And they did.

"It's like chess," their father said. "You gotta always keep your eyes open. Be on the look out for any opportunity that comes your way. And when it does," he said with a laugh, "jump on it! Be alert for whatever's next."

"That's right, Jack," his wife agreed. "The world needs more Lerts."

"You're here just in time," said the elderly Jack Rabbit who greeted them at the entrance to 'Bed, Bunk and Be Gone.' "That is if'n you're a wanting a campsite. And why else would you be here?" he chuckled. "That there family just decided to leave! Fed up with crowds, they said. And I can't say I blame them. Why in the world anyone would want to fight crowds is beyond me. But," he said smiling, "I'm sure glad they do! Gotta fill my coffers one way or another."

"That the campsite?" asked Jack, pointing to a family of Otters scurrying to and fro, grabbing tents, coffee cups, and plastic trays.

"It is," said the Hare while studying his clipboard. "You sure are lucky. Everything else is booked."

"We'll take it," said Jack.

"Of course, you will," laughed the Hare. "You ain't gonna find anything else. Are y'all here too for the...?"

"You heard about the opening of the communal feeding shed?" asked Sarah incredulously.

"The what? Don't know what you're talking about," he replied. "No, that special whatchamacallit over at Disney World. Just when you think they've done it all, they come up with some new fancy something."

"Oh," said Sarah. She stayed so busy with her own projects that she often forgot there was an outside world. But not her children. Disney's new Space Mountain had been the talk of the schoolyard. "Can we go?" they asked in unison.

"We'll see," their father said in his usual not-now-save-it-for-later tone. "First things first. We need to get settled. Where do I sign?"

"Right here," answered the Hare, thrusting the clipboard inside the station wagon. "But you'll have to wait just a bit to set up. That Otter family has certainly made quite a mess of things."

"Not to worry," said Jack. "One's mess is another's opportunity." Pulling his emergency chess set out from under the front seat, he asked, "Chess anyone?" A collective groan filled the air.

The next day, the family gathered for the grand event.

"About time you got here," said Jack's mother, forcefully pulling her son aside.

"Mother, you said it would start at 2:00, and it's only noon," he replied, pulling away from her grasp.

"There's so much to do!" she said frantically. "Like what?" asked Jack. "Well, like sweep and mop and..."

"Mother, you're seriously not wanting us to clean this feeding shed?" he asked, looking around the pristinely laid concrete and white-washed walls. "Why? There's not a crumb in site. Mice would starve to death here."

"Good," she said. "They're most certainly not welcome!"

"Mother," said Jack laughing, "I thought you said this was a feeding shed for *all* of God's creatures."

"Well, *most*. Not all. Certainly not scurry little things who can climb up and look you in the eye."

Right then, Jack heard a squeak. He looked at his mother to see if she too had heard it. She hadn't. "Should I say anything?" he wondered. "There'll be such a commotion later when everyone else is here...?"

"Stop your day dreaming and go get those youngins of yours. I've thought of a few things they need to learn," she said.

Casting his eyes in the direction of the squeak, he caught sight of a Mouse. A real, live Mouse. Not the rubber kind his children love to throw at their mother. She jumps every time, even though she knows they're not real. "Once, she even broke the chandelier," he remembered. "Hmm," he thought, "I don't think Sarah's gonna want to come in here. *Ahem*," coughed Jack, "I hate to rain on your parade, Mother, but it looks like some uninvited guests have already arrived," he said as he pointed at the wall.

Just then a Mouse stuck out its tiny little nose. "Thwack! Thwack! Thwack!" went the mop his mother slammed against the wall. "Take that, you little varmit," she screamed. "Shoo! Get out! You are *not* ruining my day!"

"Mother," said Jack, barely holding back the ripples of laughter rising up from his belly, "I think we have an even bigger problem," he said, nodding towards the far end of the room and bringing his mother's attention to the source of his complaint. A very large hole was clearly visible. A hole about the size of three croissants. And in that hole were at least fifty little Mice heads, peering out as if they were watching a show. A performance. All eyes glued on Jack and his mother.

"EEEEEEK!" she screamed, charging to the other side of the room and jamming the mop into the hole. "Out! Out! Out!" she yelled with each jab. Her form reminded Jack of an Olympic fencing contestant except that she wasn't nearly as glamorous. Spit frothed at her jagged mouth with each jab.

Despite her many jousts, there was no evidence that she had made contact with the Mice. They had simply disappeared.

"Mother," asked Jack, preparing himself for her certain volatility, "uh, did you make this single wall like I suggested?"

"No, I certainly did not! What decent feeding shed would have only *one* wall. That would mean one small hole and anything could come inside."

"Well, Mother, dear," he said cautiously, "what you've done instead is create a Mice condo. It seems to be an ideal living space for small rodents."

No response. Then suddenly his mother transformed into a Jennet Jackhammer. She was jumping in place so violently, stomping her hooves with such force, that he feared she would damage the impervious concrete floor.

"Okay," he thought to himself, "time to take another tactic." Softening his tone, he asked, "Can you try and calm down Mother?"

She did appear to actually give it a try. To calm down. The speed of her pounding lessened slightly.

"That's it, take a deep..." but before he could say the word "breath," she whacked him on the head.

"Why didn't you tell me that was why you wanted it to be single-wall!" she screamed.

"Ouch, ouch!" he yelled. "That hurts, Mother," doing his best to move towards the door. "I didn't know that's what would happen. It's just that I didn't see the need to spend more money than necessary on a...*cough*...feeding shed."

"So, you're making fun of me now. Is that it? Make fun of your poor old mother?" she said angrily. "Feeding sheds *are* important. A Donkey's got to eat."

"Yes, Mother, of course we do. It's just, it's just making them double walled and then adding a bell, and...well, don't you think that's overkill?" he asked, almost at the door.

"Overkill!" she screamed. "I'll show you overkill; I'll kill you over this!" still beating him on his head, then moving towards his back and rear. "Is that any way to treat your dear old mother?! I'm fragile, I tell you!"

Jack finally managed to make it to the door. Open it and back out. All the while trying his best to protect himself from her nonstop battering.

"Skedaddle you!" she called when he finally managed to gallop away. "And go get those worthless Mule offspring of yours. It's time to get busy! We've got to get this cleaned up before two! That's when the guests arrive!" she screamed. "The mayor's coming!" she added, stressing the word mayor as if it were God himself. "He'll be here for the blessing." And in case he hadn't heard, she yelled, "Don't forget those rotten children!"

"Yes, Mother," was all he managed to say as he escaped with his life. And sure enough, he hurried back to take care of things like he always did. Like the dutiful son that he was.

"Kids," their father said, "if you laugh, I'll kill you. For real." He then quickly filled his family in on what he had just witnessed in his mother's gleaming new feeding shed.

"Bang," he said to Marvin, and then Minnie and Molly, and finally, his wife. "Bang. You're all dead. But first, I need you to get your butts in there and help clean out those Mice."

Picking himself up off the floor, Marvin hee-hawed, "Serves her right, the old Rat!"

"Marvin," his father said, trying his best to be serious, "we've raised you to respect your elders. Now's your day of reckoning. Show me what you're made of."

"Yes, sir!" said Marvin, doing his best to stand up straight, be respectful and refrain from further gut-wrenching guffaws. "I'm on it," he said with one last, "Haaa!" busting out in spite of himself.

"And you two Mares," their father said in a serious tone, "I need you to get in there and clean things up."

"What about Marvin?" they asked.

"He'll do his bit, like he always does."

"Yeah, right," they said under their breaths. "Guess that means he won't do much of anything," whispered Minnie after they were safely out of hearing range.

"Miracles can happen," said Molly.

"Yeah, right," her big sister said with a glare as she opened the door to the shed. "When hell freezes over." And then suddenly changing her tone, she playfully sang, "Entrez-vous, Mule-masaille. Step into the grand feeding shed. A work of art. Where blessings are bestowed on creatures large and small," she laughed, emphasizing the word "small."

"Minnie!" said Molly. "You know what Dad said. Not to laugh."

"Oh, you worry wart," said Minnie. "He's not going to kill us, but *she* might!" she added, pointing to their grandmother who was heading their way. "Get busy, little sis. 'Show me what you're made of!'" she scoffed, imitating their father's command. Then picking up a mop, Minnie started beating the wall with all her might.

"Places everyone!" called their grandmother just a short while later, "Places!"

"You heard her kids," said Jack. "Hop to it!"

And as quick as a wink, all five of them lined up according to age. Jack, the Mammoth Donkey first, then his Mare wife, Sarah, followed by their Mule children: Minnie, Marvin, and Molly.

"That's it. About time your offspring showed some respect," said Jack's mother.

"They did just perform a minor miracle, Mother," he said. "All the Mice are gone. The hole's been patched. A little thank you is in order, I think."

"I don't care what you think," she snapped. "You all owe me. All of you. Without me, you wouldn't be anything. Nothing, I tell you."

"Yes, Mother," said Jack. Leaning away from his mother and towards Sarah, he coughed, "Now's not the time to make a scene."

"And when is?" she asked. "You most certainly wouldn't want to mess up her big day," Sarah said bitterly.

"Here they come!" called Grandmother before Jack could say anything else. "I see the mayor! See! He's riding on the black Stallion."

"The Pig? Your town's mayor is a Pig?" asked Jack.

"Beggars can't be choosers," she simply said. "And you *will* show him respect! All of you," taking her place at the end of the line next to Molly.

"Yes, ma'am," said only Molly. The rest of her family did their best to keep their mouths shut. No telling what might come out.

It wasn't long before all the dignitaries began streaming in. The mayor: "You must be so proud of her!" he squealed. The county council: "We're so grateful. Saved us having to build it ourselves!" they gushed. And the local community board president: "We're honored to know her. What a fine Jennet she is."

And after them came members of the community. "Thank you," Molly said over and over, shaking more hooves than she thought possible. "Thank you for coming. Yes, it *is* a lovely feeding shed."

The rest of her family was snickering. Not so secretly feeling that this whole event was a sham, farce, ridiculousness carried to the umpteenth degree.

"Let's call it what it is," thought Jack. "My mother has simply purchased accolades. Praise. A ticket to heaven. Granted, it *is* a nice feeding shed, but still. It's not the Taj Mahal. Or an orphanage that can really make a difference. That's my mother," he thought, shaking his head. "Wants everyone to know what a fine Christian she is. And the only way that's ever going to happen is to put on a show. Stage an event. All of it bought and paid for by her."

Molly, however, could see the real gratitude in everyone's face as they passed through the line. "They're actually excited about this," she thought. So again, and again, she shook hands. Paws. Hooves. Whatever it was they presented to her, she shook it. And in the midst of this monotonous afternoon, she felt Grandma Rose's presence: "She's doing her best. It's all she knows."

And every once in a while, Molly heard a squeak. Thankfully there was so much noise inside the shed that her grandmother didn't notice. Earlier that day, while cleaning out the wall, Molly had found a Mouse who was obviously in the motherly way. "I can't send her off in that condition," she had thought. Deciding to hide the pregnant Mouse even from her sister, Molly had tucked the little mother-to-be Mouse deep inside her skirt pocket. It wasn't until the next day, when Molly heard her mother's scream while sorting laundry that she remembered what she had done.

Two days later, the family of five was safely tucked away in their station wagon. Trailer attached, they were heading home. The trip to Florida and the Grand Shed Opening was over. "That was so much fun!" yelled Molly from her spot in the back. "Thanks again,

Mom and Dad," she shouted, "for letting us go to Space Mountain."

"Well," their dad said with a smile, "I figured you kids needed some kind of reward. That was quite some feat you pulled off. First, repairing the shed in time, and second, fooling your grandmother so completely. I think she really thinks you're proud of her for donating that shed."

"Who knows what she thinks," said their mother. "I'm just glad to be leaving Florida. The further I am away from your mother, the easier I can breathe."

"Me too," said Minnie.

"Me three," said Marvin.

"Me don't know," thought Molly. It befuddled her how her family continued to poke fun at their grandmother. "Sure," she thought, "she makes the Wicked Witch of the East look mild, but still...I think she was trying her best. Wanting to do good."

But Molly kept her thoughts to herself. She loved her family, but she also realized she was different. An outsider looking in. Someone who saw the world so very, very differently.

Mountain Camp
or
Close Your Eyes

"Hurry up kids," cried their mother. "We've got to get going if you want to be there in time for the first flag!"

"Coming, Mom," cried Molly, so excited to be going to camp for the first time.

"Why does Molly have to come?" asked Marvin, as unhappy as Molly was excited.

"Marvin, I've already told you," their mother scolded. "She's old enough now to be in the Indian Princess class. And that means for this one year, and this one year only, you will both be at camp together."

"Yeah! How wonderful!" he said sarcastically.

Molly chose to ignore him. Not notice. He wasn't about to rain on her parade. Derail her from her track. She had heard Minnie talk about this camp for so long, and now she was finally getting to go. She could barely contain her excitement.

"Molly," her sister had solemnly said, "when you're older, you might get to be an Indian Princess too. I'm not promising, 'cause there's only one for each cabin, and there are ten campers in a cabin. Oh, no," she added, thinking it through, "make that nine. The tenth is the counselor. But...it's possible you might be chosen. And if you are," she teased, because it was clear that she didn't really think Molly would be picked, "you get to go to a secret ritual."

But before Molly could ask any more questions, her sister had raised her right hoof to her lips, making the secret Indian Princess vow of silence that she had shown Molly about five thousand and twenty-three times. "But I promised not to tell," she said, turning and walking away.

"It'll be fine, Molly," she heard her mother say, bringing her back to the present moment. "Your brother won't bother you at camp, and you'll make lots of new friends."

"I hope so," thought Molly.

No one from her church or school would be there. Their family trip to Florida had taken place during the time allocated to their district. That meant she was joining youth from another part of the state and Molly wouldn't know anyone. Yes, she was a little concerned, but rather than worry herself sick, she decided to put blinders on and focus only on what lay directly ahead.

"It won't be much longer," her mother said, once again rousing Molly from her daydream. "We just go up and then over that mountain ridge," she said, pointing at the distant range. "It's on the other side."

Once their mother left the main highway, the road became more and more narrow. Curvy. And steep. They were climbing so high that Molly wondered if the car would slide off the mountain and into the ditch below.

"We're going to fall," Marvin teased, somehow reading her mind.

"Oh, don't be silly, Marvin" said their mother. "It's never happened before..." And then stopping herself, she remembered the flash floods when she was young. That year her group from the orphanage had not been able to attend.

"It's a beautiful day," their mother said. "Not a cloud in the sky." She was quite relieved. No rain meant that she would be able to make it back down the mountain and then on home.

"There it is!" cried Marvin as they rounded the last bend and found themselves in a wide, mountain hollow. Marvin loved camp. He too didn't care that none of his friends were coming.

"Children," their mother said as she drove onto the front lawn, "be sure and get everything out of the car. I am *not* coming back because you forgot something."

"Okay, Mom," they both said as they collected their many bags, careful not to miss a single thing.

"That's Butch!" Marvin explained to his little sister, pointing to a rather large Mole who was directing the stream of vehicles into an organized row. "He's in charge of everything. Whatever he says, you better do!" he said teasingly. Through the years Marvin had also heard his sister's stories about being chosen to be an Indian Princess. He was starting to realize the power of a taunt.

"Bye," their mother said, about to pull away. "See you in a couple of weeks!" And then, remembering the money that she had carefully set aside for their concessions, she shouted, "Here's your five dollars each. Use it wisely if you want it to last both weeks."

"Thanks!" cried Molly, tucking the bill into her pocket. Excited and scared, she wasn't really sure if she was glad to see her mother leave. "It'll be okay, kid," said Marvin unexpectedly. He didn't really mean to pick on her; it's just what older brothers did. It was so much easier to be kind when no one was watching. "I'll see you in two," he shouted as he ran up the hill to find his cabin. He was true to his word. Molly didn't catch site of him again until fourteen days later.

Left on her own, Molly wasn't quite sure where to go. She wandered around until finally, she heard, "Are you Molly?" She looked down and saw the most precious Rabbit that she had ever seen.

"Yes," Molly answered shyly.

"Great," the Rabbit said. "You're the last on my list. Come on. We're in cabin six. Right this way." Molly followed, relieved to feel her counselor's kindness.

"Okay, Molly," she said once they reached their cabin. "You and I are last, so we get to choose between these front bunks. Which do you like?"

Molly looked and sure enough, only two bunks by the door were available. An upper and a lower. The rest were piled high with all kinds of stuff. Clothing, sleeping bags, pillows.

"I'll take the lower," said Molly. The thought of crushing her tiny counselor if the top bunk were to cave in horrified her. "Wouldn't make Indian Princess that way. That's for sure."

"Great!" said her counselor, and in one easy hop she was on top of the bunk, her tall ears brushing the sloped roofline.

"Alright campers!" she called from her perch. "It's time for introductions. I'm Miss Betty and below me is Miss Molly."

Not sure whether she should be relieved that she didn't have to introduce herself or aggravated that she didn't get to, Molly simply waved.

"Don't worry about getting everyone's name right off the bat," said Miss Betty, practically hopping off her bed as she spoke. "That'll come in time. For now, I want you to unpack your things. Get acquainted with your space and your neighbors."

"Hi, I'm Barbara." "I'm Colleen." "I'm Martha." The Mares quickly exchanged hellos and unpacked their things. Their counselor's easy style inspired trust. Or were they just enchanted with her adorable bounciness? Regardless, two minutes later, they were all set.

"Great!" their counselor said again. "Molly, may I?" she asked pointing at Molly's back.

"Sure," said Molly, not sure if it was cool to already be Miss Betty's pet.

"Great!" their counselor said, hopping from her top bunk onto Molly's back. "Time to show you around."

"Whoa!" said Miss Betty whispering in Molly's ear. "I can see you're excited, but do please slow down a bit. Us Rabbits are a slippery bunch."

"Oh, sorry," said Molly blushing.

"There you go," said her counselor. "That's a nice trot."

Glancing back, Molly could see all the other Mares following in a single row.

"Where does this path go?" she wondered.

"Over there is the lake," called Miss Betty. "You'll have swimming lessons first thing tomorrow morning!" she said, yelling as loudly as she could so that everyone could hear.

"And over there," she said, pointing with her ears, "is the chow hall. See the flag?" And without waiting for an answer, she continued, "It's in front of the dining hall. You're to meet there promptly after the second bell in the morning. Got it?"

"Yes!" the Mares called out in unison.

"First bell, get out of bed," she explained. "Second, meet at the flag post. Now only good little Mares who follow all these directions will be considered for Indian Princess."

A murmur shot through the line. "Looks like the others have big sisters too," thought Molly.

The tour didn't last long. Their counselor just wanted them to get a lay of the land.

"Now, Mares," Miss Betty cried from where she now sat on a tall tree branch, "I want you to know you can come to me at any time.

If you have questions or any kind of concerns. I'm all ears. Yes, there are rules, but the main priority at camp is to have fun. Got it?"

"Got it!" they all cried, quickly learning that those two simple words made Miss Betty smile.

"Great!" she said for the thousandth time. "Follow the rules. Be kind, honest, and all will be well."

"Really?" Molly wondered. "I get into all kinds of trouble when I'm honest," she thought, remembering the many times she'd put her feet in her mouth by saying the first thing that came to mind.

"Ding. Ding. Ding. Ding," rang the bell by the flag.

"Four bells, girls," explained Miss Betty. "That means time for lunch. Show me how quickly you can get there and into place."

A deafening thunder arose as the nine Mares dashed up the hill.

"Hmm," Miss Betty wondered aloud once they had left, "Which Mare is going to be this cabin's Indian Princess?"

"Ding!" went the first bell of the day. Molly shot straight out of bed, practically knocking Miss Betty off the top bunk.

"Pail, check," Molly said to herself, grabbing her bucket from under the bunk. She then hurriedly clopped off to the bathhouse. "Wash face. Check. Brush teeth. Check. Do my business. Check. Everything back in the pail? Check." She ran back to her cabin dressing faster than any backstage artist in a Broadway play. Panting, she reached the top of the hill and got in line before anyone else. "That should do it," she thought. "I'm well on my way to becoming an Indian Princess."

This routine became her pattern for the next fourteen days. Not once did anyone beat her. Not even that prissy Miss Martha of a Mule who loved to brag how her daddy bought her everything she wanted.

"My, my, Molly," said Miss Betty when she hopped up to the front of the line for roll call. "Quite the little punctilious Mule. Wouldn't be vying for Indian Princess now, would you?" she asked.

Molly just smiled. Everyone wanted to be named Indian Princess. Even the Mares who all dressed in Goth and acted like they didn't care wanted to be named Indian Princess. They wouldn't admit to it publically, of course, but if it were offered, they'd accept!

The days continued in a comfortable rhythm. "Ding." Get up. "Ding ding." Line up. "Ding, ding ding." First activity of the day And so it continued until the sixth ding of the day and lights out.

Molly loved the routine. The consistency. And the absence of yelling. Perhaps she enjoyed that the most. No, "Clean up your room! Wait till your father comes home!" and her mother's constant refrain, "Why did I marry you anyway?"

That didn't mean that camp life was quiet. It was actually quite loud at times with all her cabin mates braying and laughing, clomping and playing. There was a peacefulness in the midst of the action. And a kindness that Molly realized she'd been missing. "How can you miss something that you didn't even know existed?" she wondered. "I don't know," she thought quietly to herself, "but I have."

And when Molly felt the pull to stop what she was doing and help the awkward Mare who obviously got her clothes from a thrift store or pick up all the pieces of a puzzle that some other Mare accidentally dropped, she realized in amazement how much she just enjoyed the moment. Being in that particular moment. "Where's that one go?" she wondered, holding an odd shaped puzzle piece. "And, wow, this one's all white? That's going to be tricky," quietly musing with herself as she picked up each and every last piece. Molly had no idea that Miss Betty was noticing her. Watching her every move.

"All the campers think it's about following the rules," Miss Betty told Miss Francesca, a gorgeous Mole and camp counselor who was careful to always have her dark shades on. "But they have no idea that it's really more about how they're being. Treating one another, including themselves."

"Yes," Miss Francesca agreed. "Mine too. They literally punch each other out of the way to be first in line, thinking that being first is what it's all about."

And so, the two weeks passed. Swimming lessons. "That's it, Molly. Keep stroking!" Art classes where the campers made such a mess that the counselors laughed themselves silly looking at their creations, colorful globs of yarn, glue, and acorns. Thank goodness Director Butch mandated the "Clean up after yourself" policy. That and the pull of the Indian Princess reward, added to the counselors' ease. Canteen time when all caution for good eating habits was thrown to the wind. Sugar coated this. Chocolate covered that. Heaps and heaps of unhealthiness that brought smiles to everyone's face. And lastly, everyone's favorite. The evening campfires.

"Okay, Mares," Miss Betty said that first evening as they were getting ready for the campfire. "There are certain rules that have to be followed." The mention of rules got everyone's attention.

"The campfire is our sacred space. We have the honor of having a full-fledged, cross my heart or hope to die Native American in our midst. He's an Eagle of the most high standing. His wings stretch out to there," she said, pointing off into the distance with her tiny, tiny paws. "We're so fortunate to have him here. I want you to treat him with the utmost respect. And actually," she said, taking a very pregnant pause, "that means not talking to him, but rather bowing politely in deference. Got it?" she asked.

"Got it," they replied in unison.

"Okay then," she said, going down the checklist in her head, "jackets, flashlights, blankets, marshmallow sticks? Yes?"

"Yes," they all replied.

"You may lead the way, Martha," said Miss Betsy. She tried her best to give every camper a chance to lead, but she didn't think they noticed. "They simply think they've done something special to deserve such treatment," she chuckled to herself.

"Thank you," Martha said, proudly trotting down the ever-darkening path as the sun set.

"I think I'll get in back," Molly decided. She liked being the very last in line. "It's quiet back here," she noticed, checking out her surroundings as they walked. "I wonder what it's like when no one is here?"

"Alright!" shouted Butch, bringing her out of her reverie. "Places everyone!" Butch was the camp director that her brother Marvin had pointed out on the first day. "We'll start with cabin one here," he shouted. "Then two, then three," he continued, pointing at the curved rows of logs, which formed a semi-circle around the campfire. Each cabin found their spot. Cabin six, Molly's cabin, was in the third row. Second from the top. "Nice," thought Molly. "Really nice view of the campfire."

Once everyone had settled into place, a quiet suddenly arose and practically knocked them over with its unexpectedness. Sure, they had all been given the speech about how they needed to be quiet and respect the native Eagle, but that they actually did it, surprised even the loudest of them all.

Silence laced only with the crackle of the fire reigned at this little amphitheater in the woods.

A few days later, when Molly was lost and trying to find her way to art class, she would stumble upon this treasure. She would realize then that it was natural. The perfect placement of rocks at the base of this sloping waterless pool could only be the thumbprint of the most master designer of all, God. The power of it had surprised her.

"Wow," she had said to no one but herself. "Wow!" A quiet rapture filled her as the sun shone down on this little piece of heaven. Molly felt more awe than she ever had in any church she had attended. Instinctually, she sat down and closed her eyes. And in those few moments of solitude, on a detour that she thought was an accident, Molly was filled with a peace which surpassed her understanding. Even richer than when Grandma Rose visited her.

Years later, she would reflect on that magic moment. That moment when God came and sat with her. Showed His presence in all that was. Is. Ever surrounding her. Ever within her.

"Molly!" cried Miss Betsy, bringing Molly back to herself. "What are you doing down there all alone?"

"Oh, nothing," said Molly, not knowing how to put into words what she had just experienced. The peace lingered as she climbed the steps to meet her counselor. Many years would pass before Molly would realize that the veneer she'd so carefully constructed around herself had begun to crack on that day. Simply by what took place in that sacred space.

"Okay, everyone," whispered Butch, bringing Molly back to the present moment. The quiet was so pervasive that his voice easily floated on the breeze like the smoke lifting off the raging fire. "I really appreciate how you've followed directions and refrained from talking."

All the campers sat up a bit taller on their logs. Proud that their effort was recognized.

"First," he continued, "we'll begin with silence. It will last for however long it lasts. I'd like you to close your eyes and focus on your heart. Ponder all that you have to be grateful for. This is private. Not to be shared."

And so, they did. To the best of their ability, they reflected on all that they had been given and experienced in their short lives.

"OMG!" exclaimed Molly to herself. She was doing her best to contain her excitement and remain silent. "I never knew camp would be so amazing!"

"Thank you, Daddy," thought Martha, "for everything you've bought me. I'm so glad we're rich."

"I'm so grateful for my cabin," thought Betty. "They don't always get along, but they somehow resolve things on their own. Thank you, thank you, thank you."

"Okay," Butch said quietly, "you can open your eyes, but please continue in your silence."

Magically, the collection of young campers complied.

"And now," he said, "what you've all been waiting for."

From the shadows came an enormous Eagle. So large. So powerful. That some of the younger campers started to cry and tremble with fear. "It's okay," Butch said softly. "You have nothing to be afraid of."

And then, in a clear, calm voice the Eagle said, "Be still, my darlings. Be still. Go inside, and you will find all the love you've ever been seeking."

"Inside where?" thought Molly, wanting so desperately to understand what he meant. "But we're outside? How can I go in if I'm out?" And then it slowly dawned on her, "He means inside myself." And so, she gave it a try. Focused on her heart and gradually began to relax.

"I remember this feeling," she thought. "Like when Grandma Rose shows up," she mused, falling into a stupor of unimaginable calm.

The silence continued for such a long time that several campers nodded off into a deep, deep sleep. Others, simply settled down. Quieted their minds. Rested. And for fewer still, the heavens opened. They were suddenly sitting in the midst of stars. All alone except for the light in the midst of darkness, encased in the purest love that they had ever felt. A love so pervasive that it felt like a second skin. A part of themselves. A love so pure they could never have imagined its possibility. For here, they felt no judgment. No conditions. Just an ever-present peace. And Molly was one of those.

"Wow!" she thought to herself. "Love! That's all there is. Love." And saying this to herself, she somehow knew it to be true.

And then, something so unexpected happened. So powerful that Molly shook from her head to her hooves. "She loves us! Grandmother loves us."

And as the truth of this filled Molly, she gave thanks to the heavens for showing themselves to her. For showing her in this split-second eternal moment of knowing that all there is is Love.

"Yes. Love is all there is. And even my nasty grandmother is full of love. She just doesn't know how to show it."

"Over here! Over here!" called Molly and Marvin's mother.

Molly couldn't believe that the last day of camp had already arrived. "Wow, where did the time go?" she wondered.

"How was it, Molly?" her mother asked, pointing to where Molly should put her bag in their small car.

"Great," Molly simply replied.

"Well, that's certainly good. Glad to hear it. And you, Marvin?"

"Fantastic!" he answered with so much enthusiasm that spit shot out of his long mouth. "I got to have Mr. Goferty as a cabin counselor. Man, oh man, can that Spider spin some webs!"

"Oh my," said their mother, not sure if she wanted to hear more.

"And did the two of you behave?" she asked Molly.

"I never saw Marvin," said Molly. "So, I don't know about him. But I did. I was a very good little Mule."

"That's nice, dear," said her mother. "How is it you never saw Marvin?"

"I don't know. We just never seemed to be in the same place at the same time. They let the Stallions eat earlier than the Mares, and then they had their own bathrooms..."

"Well, of course!" her mother said. "Sounds like a sensible way to handle a co-ed camp. Okay, you two, hop to it. We need to get this show on the road. Your father has a chess symposium, and I promised him that we three would attend."

"Great," groaned Molly, all the excitement from the past two weeks sliding out of her.

"Nothing can get *me* down," said Marvin to Molly.

"Great," thought Molly. "It's already started. Back to the same 'ole routine. Boy, I can't wait till camp comes around again next year."

"Everyone in?" asked their mother as she pulled out onto the mountain road. "Time to get you kids back to the real world."

"Ready, Indian Princess?" asked Marvin, giving her a knowing smile.

"How did he know?" Molly gasped, already far from camp.

Stop Bragging!
or
Be Ashamed of Your Self

The rest of the summer passed quickly, and Molly was soon back in school.

"Stop bragging!" said Harriet, Molly's best friend.

"What?" thought Molly, swallowing her excitement and tucking it deep into her body. "I didn't mean to," she said to Harriet.

"Well, you were," said her friend. "Not everyone can be as good a runner as you!"

Still confused, Molly thought, "Was I really bragging? I was just so excited, so thrilled to win," she didn't know what else to say. So, she turned inside and acted like she was watching the other runners. "Deep in here," she reminded herself, "no one can touch me. But...I didn't really mean to brag. Is it bad to be excited about winning?"

A sadness descended upon Molly. A sadness so all-consuming that she felt like weeping. "I just won, but I feel like crying?" she thought. "Is that how it's supposed to be?" The joy of her body, its swift movement, and her mastery quickly evaporated. In its stead came shame. Shame of her bragging. Of winning. Of how it made her friend feel.

Turning back to her friend, she asked, "Wanna head on home?"

"Sure, this is lame anyway."

"Lame," thought Molly to herself. "What I'm good at is lame."

"Hey! Let's go to the store and get some candy!" said Harriet. "I've got this money burning a hole in my pocket. I've been dying to try the new frozen Zero bar."

"Sure," said Molly, not really sure what she was feeling. "My sister loves those."

"My treat!" announced Harriet, "My treat and let's blow this joint!"

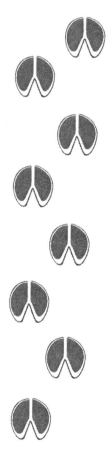

You Can't Always Have Fun: Take Two

"Molly," her father often said to her, "you can't always have fun. You have to work, work, work."

"But why, Daddy?" she asked. "Why?"

"Because that's the way the world works. You need to do well in school. Get a good job. And then save your money," he said.

"Mom doesn't work."

"You're right. She doesn't have an official job, Molly, but her work is taking care of you. The house. Haven't you noticed how much time she spends designing and changing the house?"

"Yes," said Molly, rolling her eyes. "What difference does it make if the curtains are red or blue?" A gnawing feeling told her that there was something more. More than just keeping up with the fashion of the time and making good grades. But no one else seemed to think about things like that.

"I'm going to the Crossleys," Molly told her father. Being with them felt different. Interesting. Whenever she was with them, she learned new things. There she wasn't afraid to ask questions. Wasn't told that she couldn't always have fun. "Why can't they be my family?" she wondered.

Molly's First Trip
or
Lift Off

"What do you mean she's not old enough?" asked Molly's father. "She will be in December," he said forcefully. Holding the receiver away from his head, he gave his wife a thumb's up. "I got this," he implied. She simply smiled back and continued to study the newspaper which lay across her lap.

Well, no," he said, turning his attention back to the phone. "Not until then, but it's in the same calendar year. That should be sufficient for your requirements." Again stretching the phone away from his ear, he whispered loudly, "I'm not letting them give no as an answer. Nothing's too good for my Molly!"

"Yes, dear," said Sarah, continuing to sip her tea and read the paper, one of her all-time favorite past-times. "Ah, I love this time of day," she said to no one in particular. Especially not Jack, he was too involved with the call. A moment later, she heard a "Bang" as Jack lay down the receiver.

"Well, Sarah, I did it. They're letting Molly go. She'll be the youngest, that's for sure, but she won't be the shyest. Think of it, Sarah, Molly's going to meet Moscow Mules."

Taking notice of his wife, he saw that she was reading the paper. Still. "Haven't you read enough for the day?" he asked.

"You can't ever get too much knowledge, dear. And the fashion section is so much better in Sunday's paper. How else am I to know how I'm to decorate our home? Much less dress?"

"Whatever," said Jack, getting up from his chair. "I'll be out in my office."

"Making more chess parts?"

"They're pieces," he said. "How many times do I have to tell you? Not parts. But pieces," leaving the room for his man cave. His favorite space in their house. A place where he spent thousands of hours carving, carving, and carving still. All for his love of chess.

"One Donkey's piece, is another Horse's part," she said after he left. "How could that possibly be as important as this year's colors?" she wondered.

Returning to her reading, she cried, "Oh no! I'm going to have to change all our comforter covers! Who knew cranberry red was passé? Well, Molly will certainly be happy. Blue's her favorite color."

"Hey Mom, I'm back," Molly called from outside. "It stopped raining, and there's nothing sadder than making mud pies on a sunny day."

"You could bring a bucket from the garage," her mother called, not wanting to lose this small window of peace.

"Nah," Molly said, coming in the side door. "That's no fun. Besides, Billy showed up. As soon as he arrived, the rain stopped. And...the fun went away."

"Sorry to hear that," her mother said. "I know how much you love the water. Oh," she added, just remembering Jack's phone call. "Your father's got something important to tell you."

"He does?" Molly asked. "Like what?"

"Let him tell you," her mother replied. She wasn't about to give up her peace and quiet.

"Where is he?" Molly asked.

"Out in his office. Where else?"

"Aww, Mom," Molly groaned. "If I go out there, he'll want me to play chess. I hate chess."

"Go on out. And that's an order. I was counting on a few more hours with my paper. Be a good girl, won't you?" her mother asked.

"Okay, Mom," said Molly.

'Be a good girl.' Those four words destroyed more afternoons of fun than any other four. "Be a good girl, Molly, and clean your room."

"Yes, Mom."

"Be a good girl and go fetch all the groceries from the car."

"Yes, Mom."

Molly was so tired of being a good girl. Not that it wasn't really part of her nature, but on some level, she knew that it was suffocating her. Molding her into something that she wasn't.

Of course, she did do bad things on occasion. Like that time she broke her sister's trophy. Molly couldn't stand how they had fussed over her non-stop and forgotten that Molly even existed. Or that time she swiped some change from someone's purse, so she could buy an ice cream. Or especially that time she wanted to hurt Billy. Really hurt him. "He's such a bully, and no one seems to notice." But still, the pull to please her parents was simply too strong. So, under duress of those four words, Molly left her mom in peace and went to her father's workshop.

"Oh, great. Just who I was thinking of," her father said when Molly arrived.

"I am *not* playing chess with you, Dad. I'm here 'cause Mom said you had something to tell me."

"That's right! I do. And boy oh boy, are you ever going to be excited," her father gushed.

"What is it, Dad? Just tell me."

"They're going to let you go. Even though you won't meet their age requirement until December, you're in on the trip. My gal Molly is going to Moscow! How 'bout that?"

"For real, Dad?" asked Molly cautiously. "Are you serious?" She had learned to not get her hopes up too high. "Disappointment can be a long drop."

"More serious than this Burro I'm working on," he said, proudly showing off his latest chess piece.

Molly had been begging her parents for weeks to let her go on this trip, but she hadn't *really* expected a "Yes." She knew it was a big deal. Cost plenty of money. But still...she had hoped. "Wow oh wow, that would be so amazing to get to go! Ride in a plane!" Her first. "And fly all the way across the ocean to Russia!"

What Molly didn't know was that her parents had called a little family gathering. A meeting of the minds, and she hadn't been invited. "Minnie, Marvin," their father had said, addressing her siblings, "your mother and I have called you here to talk about something important. Something that could change things, so we need to know how you feel."

"Spit it out already, Dad," said Marvin. "I'm already late for football practice," impatiently thumping his tail on the floor.

"Patience, my boy, patience."

"And if you hit my hoof one more time," said Minnie to her brother while blowing on the red polish, "I'll, I'll... "

"Now, now," said their father before she could complete her threat. "Stop provoking your brother." Turning toward Marvin he added, "That's enough! So, I wanted to get your opinion..."

"You said that already, Dad," complained Marvin.

"So I did..." Looking over at his wife for support, he took a deep breath, "Kids, how would you feel about Molly getting to take a trip to Moscow? To get to hang out with Moscow Mules?"

This trip was important to him. Molly had exhibited a wanderlust since she was born. Time and time again she would take off on her own. To the park. The store. Anywhere within walking distance. "Why are they so worried?" she often wondered. "I know where I'm going." Her father recognized her passion for travel, an urge he had also had but never been able to realize. But...he also didn't want to create dissension. Foster rivalry between the siblings.

"I don't want either of you to be jealous," their father explained, expecting to meet resistance. "So if..."

"Fine by me, Dad," said Marvin, getting up in a dash. "I've heard all about those Mules. That's the last place I'd want to go."

"Me too, Dad," said Minnie. "They're just so wild and uncultivated. Molly with her bareback will fit right in. Besides, all she wants to do is wander. Let the kid go. She'll love it."

Surprised by their easy agreement, Jack quickly recovered. "Okay then, it's all settled. Molly's going on this trip, and her mother and I will get her up north to join the group, but," he said, changing his tone to show his disappointment in his oldest daughter, "Minnie, I will *not* hear you talk about Molly's bare-back again. Just because you and Marvin have dark, dun lines running down your backs and Molly doesn't is no reason to make fun."

"Fine, fine, I'll stop," Minnie said laughing. "I didn't mean anything by it. But please, Dad, make her stop tagging along on my dates. There's nothing more embarrassing than having a little sister around when I finally get a chance to go out with a Horse stud."

"Okay, Minnie," her father replied, "I'll talk to her about it, but it saddens me that you're only interested in Horses. Donkeys are equine too, you know. I've got some friends who would love to set you up with their Jacks. But," he added, "I do understand the draw of a Horse," smiling now at their mother. "I sure do love your mother's amazing features. But..." he said, taking a moment to think about it, "since your sister won't be with you on your dates, and we can't have you go out unsupervised, your mother and I will be happy to chaperone."

"What?" gasped Minnie, even more horrified at the thought of her parents tagging along. "Just kidding," her dad chuckled. "Dad, sometimes you can be a real..." "I know honey, I'm a real Horse's Ass."

"Now be sure to put paper on the seat," her mother said for the thousandth time since they had left home.

"Yes, Mom," Molly answered. "But I'm not really sure they use seats."

"Oh, they must," her mother said with a concerned look. She wasn't quite as gung ho about this trip as her husband. "First trip alone. First time on a plane. Doesn't know anyone. Just learning the language." Her mother's list of worries was quite long.

"Don't let them intimidate you," Molly's father added, punching her playfully on the shoulder.

Molly was doing her best to put on a brave front. Sure, she was excited, wanted to go, learn the language, but also, she couldn't help but be a little nervous at the same time.

"Oh my!" someone called from a distance, bringing Molly out of her reverie. "She sure is a young one!"

"You must be Miss Mabel," said Molly's father, putting himself between his daughter and the Mule Mare carrying a clipboard. He wanted to protect Molly and play down any talk about how she was the youngest. Despite her brave front, he could see that she was nervous.

But it was too late. Molly *had* heard. She suddenly noticed how much older everyone else was. "They look like they're already in high school," she thought.

"My daughter isn't afraid of anything!" said Jack, puffing his chest in pride.

"I'm not so sure," thought Molly. "I've wanted this for so long, how could I possibly be scared? They're not all that different from Minnie or Marvin," she thought, gazing at the other participants. She was doing her best to be brave, but hearing those words, "She sure is a young one!" somehow made it all real. And she felt her age.

The quiet got Molly's attention. Looking up, she saw that they were all looking at her. Intently. Concern was written all over their faces. Her mom, her dad, and some important looking someone with a clipboard. "That must be Miss Mabel," Molly thought. And then, completely forgetting her manners, she asked, "Are you a Hinny?"

"Why, yes, dear," Miss Mabel replied. "How could you possibly tell?"

"Oh, my best friend's a Hinny. I love Hinnies!" she gushed, so happy to have something to hold onto. Not that she would be such a ninny to *literally* hold onto Miss Mabel, but Molly somehow felt that she had a friend. Every Hinny she had ever known had been kind to her. "Surely, she'll be the same," Molly hoped.

Miss Mabel blushed. Her plain tan body glowed a soft pink. Smiling at Molly, she said, "It's a pleasure to meet you." And in an attempt to comfort her youngest ward, she added, "Now, we won't be staying that close to each other, but if there's ever anything you need, anything at all, just get word to me. That's what I'm here for, to help you have the best experience possible."

And then with a smile, she turned and called to the mingling crowd, "Time to board everyone! Get your bags, say your goodbyes..."

"I promise," said Molly before her mother could even speak. "I'll always put paper on the seat. Each and every time I go to the restroom. I promise."

And then turning towards her father she added, "I'll hold my own, Dad. Really, I will," doing her best to show a confidence she didn't quite feel.

"That's my Mare," he said, pulling his youngest close and hugging her tight. It was now his turn to act brave as tears ran down his smiling face.

"Gotta go!" said Molly, quickly pulling away. And before her parents could say "Boo," Molly was in line with all the others. Mules from the North who spoke with funny accents.

"Bye, Molly!" her parents cried while waving with all their might. But Molly didn't hear. Nor see. She was already a world away. Deep in her own thoughts. "Will I make any friends?" she wondered, noticing how the others were already in groups. Pairs. Cliques. Turning back one last time, she saw that her parents had already left. Molly was all alone.

"Thank you go-spo-JHA Stravinsky," Molly said for the umpteenth time, always doing her best to correctly pronounce Mrs. in Russian. Her host family had been so nice to her. Taken her on excursions. To old cities. Big cathedrals. Even Sunday cocoa and dessert. "But when will they leave me alone?" she wondered.

"You must keep an eye on her at all times," Miss Mabel had told the family when Molly first arrived. "She's the youngest Mule in the bunch, and I can't let anything happen to her."

They were the oldest host parents. So old that others were constantly telling their birth daughter, "Your grandparents are so nice. How lucky you are!"

But sometimes Molly wished they weren't so nice. Helpful. Always watching. Always asking, "Can we get you anything? Another soda?" Molly had never drunk so many sodas in her life. "I must be putting on weight," she thought. "Don't they ever drink water?" Molly didn't want to be disrespectful, but she couldn't help thinking, "They never let me do anything. Be alone. I wish I could spend some time with the other Mules."

Finally, she got her chance.

"Children!" called Miss Mabel one day at school. "We're having an excursion."

It was such a treat to get to see Miss Mabel. She worked with the more advanced students, so Molly rarely saw her. Molly was part of the lowest level class with other students who were also just starting to learn Russian. "How are you? I'm fine," they said over and over and over. In Russian, of course. Molly didn't want to complain. She was very happy just to be there, but still, she wondered when the excitement would begin.

"Your host families won't be joining us on this excursion," Miss Mabel explained.

"Yes!" Molly said, forgetting herself for a moment and speaking her truth.

Glancing Molly's way Miss Mabel continued. "Oh no!" thought Molly. "Now I'll get into big trouble." Thousands of miles from her own parents, Molly still couldn't break the habit of wanting to be good. Do the right thing.

"I blew it," she thought. "From that one little 'yes.'"

"Quiet! Quiet!" Miss Mabel called. The students were so excited at the thought of an excursion without their host families that they had begun to chatter and ask, "Where do you think we're going?"

"I need your attention," Miss Mabel shouted. "We'll be going in groups, but not by your class, I've made new groups. They're posted over..."

Before she could finish, all the Mules dashed over to discover which group they were in.

"Yes!" said a Mule Stallion Molly had first noticed while still in the states. "He's so cute," she had told herself that day. And the next. And the one after.

"We're together, Marty!" he called to his friend.

Molly had also noticed Marty, simply because he was always by his friend's side. He wasn't as cute as the other and seemed to practically be his friend's shadow.

Eventually the crowd lessened, and Molly was able to get close enough to read the lists. "Frank, Mathilda, Ernest," she read until finally she found Molly. "And there's a Marty," she noticed. "I wonder if it's that Marty?" she thought, feeling an excitement begin to bubble up within her.

"Bus number one over here!" shouted Miss Mabel. "Two, over there! Three's on the other side!"

Molly anxiously joined her group while frantically looking to see who else was on the bus.

"Marty!" she exclaimed excitedly because that meant 'you know who' was also there.

"I think she likes you," said the cute Stallion Mule.

"Nah, do you really?" asked Marty.

"She shouted your name when she got on the bus," he said. "Didn't you hear it?"

"Yes," said Marty. "But maybe there's another Marty."

"There's *not* another Marty," he said. "I'm telling you. I think she likes you."

"If this is another of your tricks, Bob," said Marty, clearly happy that he had been noticed by a cute Mule Mare.

"It's not. I promise," said Bob.

Leaning back in his seat, Marty pondered the meaning of this. "A girl likes me. Me, Marty. They always like Bob, but she likes me," he thought excitedly. "Finally," he thought, "maybe I'll get to kiss a Mare."

"Yes, go-spo-JHA Stravinsky," said Molly from the top of the stairs, "I heard you. I'll be right down."

"Should I bring a sanitary napkin?" she asked herself for the thousandth time. "I'm almost out, but I haven't really used one yet!"

It should have been her menstrual cycle by now. Well, at least that's what she thought based on what her friends back home told her. So, every day she had been using the same worn out but not yet really used sanitary napkin. This couldn't go on forever. She just knew that the one day she didn't wear one, it would arrive. At the most inopportune time.

Taking a deep breath, Molly decided to leave it behind. "Please, God," she asked. "Please let it not happen today."

And it didn't. Not on that day. Or the next. Or the week after. Somehow Molly's cycle completely skipped her entire time in Moscow. But for Molly, the problem was that she hadn't gotten the memo. Her body gave her nary a clue. And there was no way she was going to ask go-spo-JHA Stravinsky for advice. Or even nice Miss Mabel.

Molly suffered in private turmoil the entire visit. Never knowing when or if it would arrive.

"Go Molly go! Go Molly go!" all the Mules chanted while clacking their ski poles together.

Everyone else had gone. Down the steep hill, around the bend, and into the pool of water. Molly could hear their chanting far, far below and knew she couldn't wait forever. Taking a deep breath, she pushed off before she could give it another thought.

"That's it, Molly!" they cried. "You got it! Go Molly go! Go Molly go!"

The rush of the wind caught her tail flipping it from side to side as she rushed down the hill. "Chhh, chhh, chhh," her skis went. She surprised herself at her agility, rhythm, and speed. "Don't think, Molly," she told herself. "Don't think. Just ski."

And that's what she did. Until the final turn. Something caught her eye. Something way up high. A Crow? Or Hawk? A flying Frog?

"What's Minnie's teacher doing here?" she thought. And in that split second, she lost it. Her focus was gone. Her legs were flying in four different directions. Her skis clicked off, continued their course and entered the pool gracefully.

"Oh no!" thought Molly, suddenly catching flight, tumbling, and curling into a ball.

"Splash!" She landed in the freezing cold water.

"Way to go, Molly!" someone cried.

"Did you see that?" another asked. "She did a somersault with a half twist!"

The cheering was so loud that Molly could hear it from under the water where she lay in a confused heap. But she was hearing out of her left ear only. Not her right.

"What just happened?" she wondered, so disoriented that it took her several moments to find her footing. Finally, she stood up and shook off the cold, cold water.

"Molly! Molly! Molly!" a crowd of Mules from all over the globe chanted.

"Best landing ever!" kind Miss Mabel said while placing a wreath around Molly's neck.

"What?" Molly asked, still not understanding what had just happened. "Did I win?" she wondered. "How?"

"Whatever made you think of that, Molly?" Miss Mabel asked. "Absolutely brilliant. Everyone else just glides in. That kicking off of the skis and doing a somersault was utterly amazing," she gushed.

Molly stood there stunned. They weren't laughing. They weren't jeering. They were cheering. For her. "How could that possibly be?"

"Let's get you out of the cold, my dear," said Miss Mabel, nodding to her assistant to cover Molly with a blanket. "And how about a warm cup of cocoa?" she asked.

"What?" Molly asked again, not realizing that she could no longer hear out of her right ear. That accidental act of grace, in the form of a somersault, had knocked the titanium pin that Dr. Gruff had placed in her ear long ago out of whack.

"Dad!" cried Molly into the phone.

"Yes," he replied from the bottom of a well. "Is that you, Molly?"

"Yes, Dad," she said, relieved that the amount of time for the call to go through had only been four hours, rather than the expected six. "I have something to tell you."

"What?" he asked. "Speak up, Molly, I can't hear you."

"My ear, Dad. I've busted my ear," she said.

"You've got a boil on your rear?" he asked.

"No, Daddy," she cried. "I busted my ear!"

"Molly, you called all the way from Moscow to tell me about a boil on your rear!" he shouted. "We're not made of money, and this is costing a fortune."

"Yes, Dad," she said softly. "I'm sorry I called."

"Don't be sorry," he said. "But you can make it up to me by playing chess when you get back. And be sure to bring something special for your mom. She deserves it, putting up with all my crap."

"Yes, Dad," said Molly again. "I will."

"And take care of that boil!" he shouted. "You wouldn't want it to get..."

"Click." He had hung up. Or the money had run out. Regardless, the line was dead.

"Hey Molly!" cried the coolest Mare of the bunch. "Come on over and hang out with us."

"Could I be hearing this right?" wondered Molly. Sometimes she wasn't sure what others said.

"Come on over!" the cool Mare said again.

"Wow," thought Molly, "I must have heard right."

She walked over quickly, but not so quickly that she looked desperate. "Be cool," she told herself. "Be cool." Smiling at the gang of hip Mule Mares, she said, "Hi, y'all."

"Wow! That was some move you did last week on the slope," said the coolest Mare of all.

Back in the states Molly had noticed this particular Mare even before they boarded the plane to Moscow. "How is it that some Mares are just so cool? So popular without even trying?" she'd wondered.

"How did you ever think of it?" Miss Cool Mule asked further.

Blushing, Molly was about to say, "Well, it was an accident really. I tripped and..."

But before she could, the cutest boy Mule and his friend, Marty, shouted, "Hey Mares, how about we go catch the train to town?" Suddenly, Molly was forgotten. The others rushed to the Stallions' sides. "What do you say?" Miss Cool Mule asked her friends, "Sounds like fun. Let's go!"

Molly turned to leave. She knew her host parents would never let her go.

"Hey, Molly!" someone called, rushing up behind her. "Aren't you coming too?"

It was Marty. The nerdy friend of Mr. Cute.

"What's he want?" she wondered. But rather than continuing to walk away, something inside her made her stop. And listen.

"Come on!" he cried again. "The train's leaving. There's just enough time to get tickets."

"Who are you kidding?" she asked herself. "You can't go. They'd be furious. Besides..." she said, not realizing that she was now speaking out loud, "I don't have any money."

"I do," said Marty. "I've got plenty. My parents are loaded."

And in less time than it takes a Hummingbird to buzz on by, Molly decided to go, throw caution to the wind, or at least any worries about her host parents. "I'd love to!" she said. "Why, thank you, Marty."

Beaming, he led the way to the station. Molly had to hold herself back, so slow was his trot. She could have easily shot past, but some invisible force was holding her back. Letting him be first. The pain she had felt so long ago after easily beating her father in a hoof race, but then having to suffer his cool disapproval, was so deeply buried that she no longer remembered her short-lived victory and initial joy.

The train ride back to the village came too soon for Molly. She'd had her best time yet on this short, student-only excursion.

"That was so much fun!" said Elizabeth, the cool Mule Mare. Molly finally had the chance to learn her name. "We're so glad you joined us, Molly. We all thought you were stuck up or something, but you're alright."

"Thanks," said Molly blushing. She had never gotten to hang out with the cool older kids. Her brother Marvin always made sure of that.

"Why haven't you been coming to the parties?" asked another Mare.

"My host parents won't let me," Molly replied. "They've been told to keep an eye on me 'cause I'm the youngest."

"Awww, if that's all," said Elizabeth, "you don't need to worry. We're staying with the head host family."

"Yeah," said another who was rooming with Elizabeth. "They let us do whatever we want! We'll take care of it."

Molly felt a glow in her heart that she hadn't felt in a long time. She didn't speak for the rest of the ride, happy just to be in the midst of their coolness. Listen to their laughter. Laugh along from time to time and wonder how in the world she got herself in this most wonderful mess.

One More Time
or
The Things That
Ants Can Do

Soon after she returned to the states, Molly visited Dr. Gruff. A second ear surgery was in order.

"Okay, Molly," asked Nurse Florence, "remember the drill?"

"Yes," said Molly, "I do. Can I please have extra blankets like last time?"

"You can, but it's good you left your stuffed toy at home. They're not allowed at the adult hospital."

"I know," said Molly. "It's okay, but I definitely don't want to see that long needle this time. In fact," she thought, "I'll just close my eyes. Imagine I'm somewhere else. In the mountains at camp. Yes, that's a good place. Back when I was a little Mare..."

Before Molly could complete the picture and remember how it felt to be there, the nurse announced, "All done."

"Really?" asked Molly. "That wasn't so bad."

"Good. The doctor will be in soon. Just relax, and it'll be over before you know it."

It wasn't quite as quick as all that, but still, it was fairly easy. Yes, Molly had to hold onto the operating table again throughout the entire surgery. It was either that or be wrapped up so tightly that it felt like being buried in sand. A lonely head for the doctor to poke and prod.

There was also the added highlight of a light scolding from Doctor Gruff. "Now how did you break this pin again?" he asked. Molly knew he wouldn't really bother to listen, so she made up a story. "I was having a picnic, and this colony of fire Ants crawled into my ear. I think it was the flying acrobatics that did it. They were celebrating..."

"Well," he said, "next time do be more careful," bringing her story to an abrupt halt.

"Right," said Molly. "Will do." And closing her eyes again, she thought, "Maybe it's time to revisit camp."

A few short hours later, she realized that she was already in her hospital room. The surgery was over. "You should be grateful I'm your doctor," she heard. "That was quite some break. I had to use an extra-long pin and really only had a nub of a stapes to work with."

"Yeah for the nub!" thought Molly, happy to be able to hear again.

"Did you hear what I said, Molly, dear?" the doctor asked. "You're so lucky to have me as a doctor."

"Yes," Molly nodded. "I am."

"Well," he said, "you must be tired from the surgery. Get some rest, and I'll be back to check on you in a few hours."

Turning on her side with her back towards the door, Molly fell into a deep, restful sleep.

The Later Years:
Almost Dry

Will You Go With Me?
or
How Dumb *Is* a Piece of Gum?

"There he is, Molly. Go up and ask him!" said Harriet, pushing Molly into the center of the hallway.

And before Molly could take another breath, she was face to face with one of the cutest Horse Stallions at the school.

"Uhh," she stuttered, "I wanted to ask if you'd like to go to the Sadie Hawkins dance with me?"

He looked her in the eyes, blinked, and turned away. Horrified, Molly ran over to her friend.

"Did you see that? He didn't say anything? It was like I wasn't even there!" exclaimed Molly.

"Could he hear you?" asked Harriet. "I couldn't."

"Oh!" gasped Molly. "Maybe I didn't say it out loud! I've been practicing for so long that I must have forgot to say it out loud," she cried.

"Don't worry about it, Molly. He may be cute, but he's dumber than a doorbell, floor mat, piece of gum. You're better off just going with all of us," she said, motioning for some friends to come over.

"Yeah, Molly, join us!" said one of Harriet's classmates, "We're going to have a slumber party after at my house. You're welcome to come." "Aww," said Molly. "Thanks, y'all. That'd be really nice."

Molly's Worries
or
Important Stuff

"What do you think happens when we die?" Molly asked her longtime friend Betsy.

"I don't know," she replied. "Why do you ask?"

"Well," said Molly, "don't you ever worry about that? What it will be like?"

"Not too much," her friend said honestly.

"Aren't you scared?" Molly asked.

"Molly, we're young. That's not going to happen for a long, long time," said Betsy.

"I wonder," thought Molly. Sometimes she just couldn't help worrying about what would happen. Could happen. All the scary things that her parents constantly warned her about. All the dangers in the world. The hereafter seemed scarier still.

"You're the only one I know who talks about stuff like this," said Betsy.

"Really?" asked Molly.

"Yes," her friend said.

"What do you usually talk about?" asked Molly.

"Oh, I don't know," said Betsy. "Like, like, who's going to the dance. What you're wearing. Important stuff like that."

"Important stuff," said Molly.

"Yeah," said Betsy. "Important stuff."

Molly didn't know what to say, so she decided to just say nothing. "No wonder I don't really fit in anywhere. That stuff is so boring," she thought to herself.

"I gotta get home," said Betsy.

"Okay," said Molly. "See you tomorrow at school."

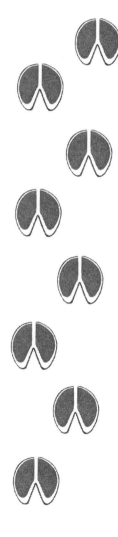

High School English
or
A Rose by
Any Other Name

"Can you read this, Marvin?" asked Mr. Tafferty, his teacher for Shakespearean studies and a very well-educated Toad.

"No," he said. "What is it?"

"Your sister's paper."

"Oh," Marvin laughed. "Looks more like a kindergartener's."

"Well, I wouldn't go that far, but yes, it needs some work," the teacher said. "Can you take a look and see if you can decipher it?"

"Well," said Marvin hesitantly, "I'll try, but I'm not making any promises."

"That's all anyone can ever do," he said. "Try their best." And with a smile he added, "Thanks Marvin."

Marvin took the paper, which was neat, un-crumpled, but filled with scrawls that looked more like Chicken scratchings rather than a high school students' handwriting.

"Upon the way of thee, I seek, of Shakespeare she doth quoteth," he read. "Huh?" he asked, scrunching up his face. Turning the pages quickly, Marvin went directly to the end. "Whenceforth he came that is her answer."

"What the?" he thought, getting up from his desk and returning the paper to Mr. Tafferty. "Sorry, I couldn't make heads nor tails of it," he said.

"Thanks for trying, Marvin."

"You're welcome," he said, not really sure how to react and if he should say anything to his little sister.

He didn't have to. During the last class of the day, Mr. Tafferty called Molly's coach. "Will you please excuse Molly from track? I need to talk to her about something that's much more important than running."

"Sure," her coach replied. "I'll send her right up."

To the coach, nothing was more important than running, but...if one of his runners didn't make the grade, they could be pulled from meets. Disqualified. Permanently. So as much as Molly's coach cracked the whip at the racetrack, he also used it for their class work. "I expect you *all* to be star pupils," he often said. "Set the standard for everyone else to follow. And make it high."

So, her coach quickly complied. "Molly in there?" he asked while standing by the door to the girls' dressing room. "She's changing," someone called. "Tell her to head on up to Mr. Tafferty's room. He needs to talk to her about something. And oh," her coach added, "she can just come on out to the track after."

"Wonder what this is about?" thought Molly as she trotted through the school. As soon as she entered her English teacher's empty room and saw her paper laid out on his desk, she knew.

"Thanks for coming in, Molly," Mr. Tafferty said while entering the room. He went straight to his desk and picked up her paper. "What's this?" he asked.

"My paper?" Molly asked.

"Yes," he said. "But what is it? What were you trying to say?"

"Well," said Molly shyly, "that Romeo and Juliet were not sure what they should do because they came from families that hated each other. But they loved each other. They didn't want to be part of their families' feud," she said.

"Okay," Mr. Tafferty said. "Then why didn't you write that?"

"Because it's an English paper," she answered.

"And what is that supposed to mean?"

"That you speak in dressed-up fancy language, kind of like in the Bible or in Shakespeare."

"No, you don't, Molly," he said. "You write like you speak."

"You can do that?" she asked incredulously.

"Yes," he replied. "How else can anyone understand you?"

"Oh, gosh, golly, thank you, Mr. Tafferty!" Molly gushed. "I've always been so scared of writing because I hadn't learned to talk all formal like."

"And neither have any of the other students," he said kindly. Hopping up on a bookshelf so he could be at eye level with her, he said good naturedly, "Molly, my dear, just write from your heart. Write how you see it. *Feel* it. And everything will work out just fine."

"Thank you, Mr. Tafferty," she said with a curtsey. "He knows so much for being so small," she thought. "Thank you!" she said again, dashing out the door, already warming up for track practice.

"What do I write on each card, Mr. Tafferty?" asked Molly the next day after school.

"It's on the board," he answered.

"Oh," she replied, "I see it now." After a few more minutes of focused work, she stopped and raised her head. "Thank you so much for helping me with this, Mr. Tafferty. It's just all been so confusing."

"My pleasure, Molly," he croaked. "I can see that you're really trying and with a little more effort, you'll come out on top."

Another hour passed in silence. Seeing that she was well on her way, her teacher got up from his chair. "Oh, I guess I'd better go," said Molly, pushing her chair back.

"No, no," he replied. "Take your time. I'm just heading down to the teachers' lounge for a break. If I'm not back before you've finished, just close the door on your way out. And oh," he added before leaving the room, "if you still need some assistance, just let me know. We can take it up tomorrow after school."

"Oh, thank you," said Molly relieved. She did still have some questions, but they were for the next step in the process, and she wasn't quite ready to ask. "Thank you so much for helping me."

"You'll do fine, Molly," he said from the hallway. "You'll do just fine."

Why Am I Kissing Him?
or
The Best Friend Ever

"Why am I kissing him?" Molly wondered. She was enjoying the playful romp in spite of herself. "I don't even like him," she mused as she felt his tongue reach further into her mouth. "And what will Betsy think?" she thought guiltily. "She's been such a good friend for so long. How can I do this to her?"

Finding strength in the midst of her remorse, Molly pulled away.

"What's wrong Molly?" asked Tommy, an adorable Horse Stallion.

"The cutest ever," thought Molly. "And Betsy's boyfriend. Not yours," she told herself with force. And yet, she couldn't bear the thought of him not liking her.

"Nothing, Tommy," said Molly simply. "Nothing at all. You're a great kisser. It's just, it's just..."

"What can I possibly say to get out of this mess?" she wondered.

"It's just that I've got to be going. I promised my mom I'd be back in time to put out the garbage," she lied.

"Lame!" she silently shouted to herself, "Lame! Molly, couldn't you have thought of something else?"

"Oh, well, okay," said Tommy, obviously disappointed. "Mules," he thought. "They're a moody bunch. You just can't ever tell what they're thinking. Mom was right, best to stick with my own kind."

Just a few days before when learning who her son was dating, his mother had exploded. "Whatever are you thinking? A Rabbit for a girl friend? Nothing can come of it. Nothing!"

"We could adopt, Mom," he'd replied, thinking of social studies class. "The teacher was telling us the other day about all the poor animals abandoned after floods and fires, and..."

"You are *not* adopting bunnies. Or dogs. Or..." she had said in a shrill voice, rising to a crescendo, "Cats! No son of mine, who I've poured my heart and soul and good upbringing into is going to marry outside of his species. No siree, Bob," she had shouted with such force that Tommy had practically buckled to his knees.

"Mom, I'm Tommy. Not Bob," he had meekly replied.

"Tommy, Bobby, whichever son of mine you are, you are *not*. Do you hear me? You are *not* marrying outside of our species," she had said with such finality that Tommy hadn't dared make a peep. Or a neigh. He'd been literally struck speechless.

"But Molly," he thought now, coming out of his reverie, "well, she's the same species, right? Why not give it another go?"

"Tommy!" yelled Molly, pushing him away after his sudden advance. "I've really got to go," she called as she quickly trotted away. "See ya!"

"What was I thinking?" she thought as she dashed towards home. Bumping into trees. Dropping her books. Molly was a mess.

"Molly!" she suddenly shouted. "Get a hold of yourself!" So, she did. She stopped and took a deep breath. And then another. By the third, she was beginning to calm down.

"Oh! I'm so sorry, Betsy," she cried. "What was I thinking?"

"You weren't," the little voice inside her said.

"No, I guess I wasn't. It was just, well, it was just, he gave me that look, and I couldn't help myself."

For as long as Molly could remember, she couldn't stand not being noticed.

"When did it start?" she wondered as she slowly drifted along a forest trail that ran behind her neighborhood. "In grade school? With Miss Granger? No," she said, shaking her head. "Definitely not. I tried my best *not* to be noticed."

Completely oblivious of a flock of birds swarming the maple trees, she continued to review her personal database of memories, stopping at Sunday School. "No," she thought. "That doesn't seem right."

And then it hit her. "It's only when I'm around boys! It's like a switch goes off. And I just have to have them see me. Notice me."

It didn't need to be grand. A simple smile would do. But somehow, some way, Molly needed to be noticed. Acknowledged.

"Wow," she thought. "I've been like this my whole life. Or," she mused, "as long as I can remember. But Betsy? How could I do this to her?"

Walking in circles, Molly was worrying herself sick. And then, as easy as pie, the solution came to her. "I'm just going to act like it never happened. Ignore it, and it'll go away."

And that's what she did. For the next few weeks, she simply avoided Tommy. He came this way. She went that way. He entered the lunch room. She left by another door. "I don't have to explain myself," she thought. "Deal with it in any way." And it would have been perfect, except for when Betsy began to complain. "He won't even talk to me," she told Molly. "I don't know what happened. One minute we were talking about where we wanted to go eat before the dance, and the next, he's acting like I don't even exist."

"I'm so sorry," Molly told her friend. Of course, she didn't say what she was *really* sorry for. That would have caused all kinds of problems that she wasn't ready to face.

"But why did he dump her?" Molly wondered. "That makes no sense. It only happened those two times."

Not sure what to do and feeling more remorse than she thought possible, Molly decided to crack open her piggy bank. "It won't make what happened go away," she thought. "But it can't hurt."

"Wow! Thanks, Molly!" cried Betsy after enjoying a big bite of her hot fudge sundae. "Ice cream's my favorite. And ice skating too! Wow! You're the best friend ever!"

I Want to Hold Your Hoof
or
Whose Life Is It Anyway?

"How in the world did I get in this mess?" wondered Molly.

It hadn't seemed like such a bad idea at the time to say "Yes" to a neighborhood Stallion's invitation to the high school dance. "How bad could it be?" she had thought.

"Bad," she was learning. "Really, really bad."

"Hey, Molly!" called Harriet from across the gym. "Love your dress!"

"Thanks!" said Molly as she waved back. "Help!" she then silently mouthed. But Harriet had already turned away. "Darn!" thought Molly. "She could have come to my rescue."

It had taken Molly's date over an hour to get up the courage to hold her hoof. So, once he did, he was not about to let go. "Want some punch, Molly?" he asked. "Sure," she replied. "Now's my chance to get away!" she thought. But he wasn't taking a chance.

He continued to hold on and dragged her over to the refreshment table. "It feels like we're attached by super glue!" she thought.

It didn't even occur to her to simply say, "Please let go of my hoof." To Molly that would have been impolite. She could feel how nervous he was just to be with her on this date. Somehow *his* feelings were more important to her than her own.

They sipped their punch while staying connected. "I'd like a refill," said Molly as soon as she finished. After their third glass and before she could ask for another, he pulled her onto the dance floor.

"Great," she thought. "Just what I was trying to avoid."

"Hey, Molly!" her friend Betsy called from her perch on the cute Horse Stallion Tommy. She was grinning from ear to ear, so happy that he had called her at the last minute to re-invite her to the dance. "How's it going?"

"Can't you see?" Molly mouthed. "It's horrible; he won't let me go!" she said, raising her hoof. And his. Betsy could see the determination in his face. He was not about to let her friend go. "Just tell him you have to go to the bathroom," Betsy suggested. "Great idea!" whispered Molly. "Why didn't I think of that?" she wondered.

So, before the slow dance music was even close to being finished, Molly announced that she had to go to the restroom. "Oh," her date replied, blushing. Regretfully, he let her go.

"Shew!" said Molly as she stepped away. Right then, Tommy turned with the beat of the music. They made eye contact. Nothing was said, but Molly was sure that she had turned purple. "Thank goodness it's dark in here," she thought as she ran off towards the girls' locker room.

The rest of the night she hid from her date. Behind her big brother, Marvin. "Go away! You're cramping my style!" Behind the stage curtains. "You're not allowed up here," a teacher called. "Move along!" And even under the punch table when she saw no other alternative. "Molly?" asked Mr. Tafferty. "Is that you?" He was the official high school dance chaperone. "What are you doing under there?"

"Oh, I dropped a contact," she quickly lied.

"Well come on out. I can't have any hanky-panky on my watch."

"Then you've got nothing to worry about," Molly answered. "But," she asked, remembering how helpful he was in class, "could I maybe have a ride home?"

"Sorry, Molly. Against school policy. Why don't you get a ride with your brother?"

"Oh, no, thank you," she said apologetically. "That wouldn't work. I've already cramped his style enough for the night. I'll find a ride." Slowly, she pulled herself out from under the table.

"There you are!" her date called. "I've been looking for you all night. It's time to go. I have to get my mom's car back by 10:00."

"Looks like I've got a ride after all," Molly said to Mr. Tafferty. Turning towards her date, while being extra careful that he didn't see her crossed hooves, she lied, "Too bad you have to return the car so early."

As they walked outside, she kept a safe distance, "No way I'm going to let that happen ever again."

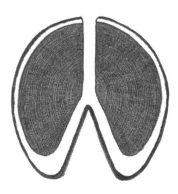

Molly's BFF
or
Molly, Can You See Me?

"Come on in," said Harriet as she pulled Molly inside and practically off her feet. "It's freezing out there! And I've got something soooo cool to show you!"

"Brrrr," said Molly, pulling off her boots, hat, coat, and parka, getting down to just her cozy fleece, tights, and sweats. "I am so glad to get out of the house. Mom and Dad are having one of their shouting matches."

Harriet smiled a look of understanding, but Molly knew her friend could never really understand. "Harriet is so lucky," she thought. "Her parents like each other. As in really, not just for show." And with a shrug and a sigh, Molly did her best to cast off all that yuckiness and enjoy the tranquility of her best friend's home.

"You were brave to cross the tracks on a day like today," said Harriet.

"It was fine," said Molly. "I just had to wait a while. I love cabooses; they're so cute."

"I like the engine," said Harriet. "They get to blow the whistle."

"That's true," said Molly. "But I'm glad I missed it today. It was a long enough wait as it was."

"It's a wonder your ears didn't freeze! Let's go to my room. It's warmer in there," said Harriet, pulling her pal into her bedroom and closing the door for privacy. "Why don't you make yourself comfortable?" she laughed after Molly had already jumped up on her lavender colored bed and snuggled into the many fluffy pillows. "You are in for a treat!" her friend said.

"What is it?" Molly asked. She'd been dying to know ever since Harriet's call. "Why didn't you just tell me over the phone?" "Because then that brother of mine might take it! And this is just for us," she said, pulling a mossy green book out from under her bed. "*Animal Totem,*" she read solemnly in such a soft voice that Molly could barely hear her.

"Why are you whispering?" whispered Molly.

"Because, it's just so cool! I want to keep it for ourselves," said Harriet, still careful to keep her voice low.

"Where did you find it?"

"At the used book store. Mom wanted something special for Dad, but she didn't want him to know she'd gone looking. So, I went shopping for her and found this little gem for me," carefully dusting it off. "I don't think it's been opened for practically forever, it had so much dust on it."

"What makes it so special?" asked Molly, not quite getting why her friend was so excited.

"It's all about animal totems!" she gushed. Seeing Molly's confusion, she added, "Totem. Not poles, though some poles have totems on them." Molly clearly still didn't understand. "Totems are animals that guide you. Speak to you. Help you," her friend said.

"Oh," said Molly. "That sounds cool."

"And not everyone has the same totem. Mine, well, mine is the Owl," she said.

My Life as a Mule

"Makes sense," said Molly. "I think you're the wisest Mule I know. Your family too."

Molly loved spending time at Harriet's house. "They're just so cool!" she thought. But most everyone else thought they were uncool. They lived on the other side of the tracks. Had a tiny house before that was "in." Drove very old cars, also before that was considered hip. Molly wouldn't ever have admitted it to her own family, but she really felt more at home there than at her parents' house. "They're all so smart, curious about life," thought Molly. "I'm always learning new things whenever I go there."

"Ah, we're nothing special," said Harriet.

"Oh, but you are!" said Molly. She was careful not to gush too much. She didn't want to embarrass herself. Also, she worried, "They might not invite me back. And if that happened, I don't know what I would do!"

"So," said Harriet, choosing to ignore her friend's obvious embarrassment, "what you do is think about what animal you see all the time. Not just every once in a while, but one that pops up all the time. Then, after you've thought about it, you look in this book for what it means." Putting the book aside, she said, "Now close your eyes, Molly, and think about it. What animal do you see most often?"

Molly closed her eyes so tight that it started to hurt. "Relax, Molly," laughed Harriet. "You don't need to be so worried. It'll come to you."

"Relax," Molly told herself. "Relax." She began to focus on her heart like Harriet had previously taught her. "This is something you can do when you're stressed," her friend had said. "Your heart is the source of all love," she'd also added. "Inside you. Inside me.

174

We all have it. We've just forgotten."

Molly had tried it a few times, but then she'd forget. "I'll have to try and remember," she told herself every time.

Once again, Molly focused on her heart and did her best to relax. "This isn't easy," she thought.

"Don't try so hard, Molly," her friend said gently. "Take a deep breath. That can help too."

Molly took such a deep breath that her friend laughed, "Not that deep. You'll hyperventilate!"

"Okay," said Molly, taking another breath but more gently this time. And then another. "What's that heat?" she wondered. All of a sudden, her chest felt like it was on fire. But she continued to try and relax while also focusing on her heart. After a short eternity, something shifted. The heat went away, and a calmness arose in its place. "Ahh," she sighed. "Dear God," she silently said, "Thank you for Harriet."

"That's it, Molly," said Harriet. "You're doing great."

A few seconds later, Molly said with surprise, "A Spider! No, lots of Spiders. That's what I'm seeing, Harriet. They're *always* around me. All the time. My bed. In the bathroom. Everywhere!" she exclaimed. "But," she asked worriedly, "does that count? As an animal?"

"Sure, it does," her friend said reassuringly. "When you're ready, we can look it up. But take your time. There's no rush."

Molly chose to keep her eyes closed a little longer. She luxuriated in the peace emanating from her heart. The expansive calm. Again, she told herself, "I have to try and remember this." But she knew she wouldn't. She knew she'd forget.

When she did finally open her eyes, she saw that her friend had propped the book up in front of her. It was open at the section on Spiders with a large drawing of a Spider at the top of the page.

"Ooo," she said, chills running up and down her spine, "Why does my totem have to be so creepy? Owls are cute and fuzzy."

"It doesn't matter," her friend laughed. "And besides," she said, pointing to the drawing, "Spiders have fuzz too. It's just harder to see. You have to get kind of close."

"I can see just fine," said Molly, not wanting to get any closer to this very detailed drawing. She wasn't sure what to think. "Spiders?" she wondered. "Why does my totem have to be a Spider? And what if it says I have to kill my husband one day? That would be awful!"

Harriet could clearly see that her friend was uncomfortable.

"Shall I read it to you?" she asked. "Yeah," said Molly with relief. "That would be great."

Once Harriet was sitting comfortably on the floor with her back against the wall, she began to read, "*Spider Totem*. The Spider is a totem for only a special few. See!" she cheered. "I told you that you were special."

"Does it really say that?"

"Yes," said Harriet, holding up the book so Molly could see.

"Wow. It's true."

"Of course, it's true," laughed Harriet. "Would I lie to you?"

"Well. Maybe. Just to make me feel better."

"Ah shush. I don't need to lie to make you feel better. Besides, that's your job. Don't make me responsible for your happiness," her friend scolded. "I've got enough to take care of just taking care of me."

"Okay," said Molly dejectedly.

"And don't get into a pity party on my account!" her friend added. "Seriously, Molly. You just don't seem to realize how talented you are."

"Can you just read the rest of it?" asked Molly. It made her uncomfortable when Harriet said nice things about her.

"The Spider represents dormant potential," her friend read. "Once activated, Spiders can weave webs of unlimited scope. Both in size and subject matter."

"What's that mean? Dormant potential?" asked Molly.

"It means that you can do lots of things. You have a lot of potential. Just like I was saying. It fits perfectly!"

Ignoring her, Molly asked, "But that word dormant?"

"It has to be activated. Like a volcano is dormant until it isn't.

And then it's spewing hot lava all over the place."

"You're saying I'm going to erupt?"

"No, you're going to weave. All kinds of webs."

"Read it again," Molly commanded. Catching herself, she added with a smile, "Please?"

"Sure," said Harriet. "The Spider represents dormant potential. Once activated, Spiders can weave webs of unlimited scope. Both in size and subject matter."

"Once activated," repeated Molly slowly. "What do you think that means?"

"I'm not sure," said Harriet. "I think that's something you'll have to discover on your own."

"And that last part?" asked Molly.

"Once activated," she read slowly, carefully emphasizing each word, "Spiders can weave webs of unlimited scope. Both in size and subject matter."

Both Mares felt the weight of these words. And in silent agreement, they withdrew to the private space within themselves where they could reflect on the deeper meaning.

Harriet was the first to break the silence. "Molly, that means nothing can limit you. Hold you back. Nothing."

"Wow," was all Molly managed to say as she wondered if this were true.

"There's more," said Harriet.

Skimming through the rest, she paraphrased. "It says that when you're seeing lots of Spiders, it means that you're NOT living up to your potential. That you could be doing so much more."

But before Molly could reflect further, Harriet's mom knocked on the door. "Girls!" she called. "I've made hot cocoa. Come on out before it gets cold!"

"Yum!" said Harriet, suddenly forgetting her precious book and dashing towards the kitchen.

But Molly hadn't forgotten. She picked up the book and read the last part. "The sighting of a large quantity of Spiders at one time represents the lack of fulfilling one's potential. The dormant potential has not yet been activated and as such cannot be fully realized."

Deep in thought, Molly hugged her friend's book to her chest and repeated out loud, "Has not yet been activated and as such cannot be fully realized."

"Molly!" her friend called. "Come on! The marshmallows have already melted!" Lured by the promise of warm chocolate sweetened with marshmallows, Molly tossed the book on her friend's bed and dashed out the door.

"Are you really going to eat all that?" asked Molly. She and her BFF had met for lunch at a fast food restaurant.

"Yeah, and what about it," said Harriet as she sat down with her tray.

"I mean *two* sandwiches ..."

"*Four* sandwiches," her friend corrected.

"Okay, four sandwiches. But fries, milk, a shake, *and* an apple pie?" asked Molly incredulously.

"I'm hungry."

"I can see," said Molly.

"Is that *all* you're going to eat?" her friend countered.

"Yes, a plain English muffin and milk is all I need."

"I'm not talking about need. I'm talking about hunger. Aren't you hungry?" Harriet asked.

"Sure," she answered. "But this is enough."

"On a diet?"

"No, I'm *not* on a diet," said Molly defensively.

"Molly," said her longtime friend, "you look fine. You don't have to worry about a thing. Your figure's perfect."

"Well," said Molly, "I don't want it to become a problem."

"Eat like that and you *will* have a problem. We have to eat, Molly."

"As you keep reminding me." Eager to change the subject Molly asked, "Do you want to go with me to church tonight?"

"No," said Harriet. "I've got too much homework. And those college admission forms are killing me."

"Oh yeah," said Molly. She tried to forget that her best friend was graduating before her. That she would be gone next year.

"Don't look so sad," said Harriet. "I'll come back on weekends."

"Yeah, right," said Molly. "Just like Minnie said she would and never does. And just like Marvin said he would. I think they like it better there, and I can't blame them. But...it has actually gotten a little better with them gone. Mom and Dad don't fight so much."

"That's good," said Harriet. "What's the topic tonight anyway?"

"Atonement," said Molly. "And salvation, redemption. We're learning how to evangelize so others won't go to hell."

"Hmm," said Harriet.

"I've tried to evangelize to you, but it hasn't worked," said Molly.

"And it won't," her friend laughed.

Harriet's family didn't go to church, but every once in a great while she would go with Molly to some church function. Roller skating. Tubing in the mountains. She even went to a beach camp once.

"Thanks, but no thanks," said Harriet.

"Why not?" asked Molly.

"I don't know exactly. It's just not my cup of tea."

"Don't you worry about going to hell?" asked Molly.

"No, not really. I don't think God is all vengeful like they say at your church."

"How do *you* think God is?" asked Molly.

"Love. I think God is simply love."

"Well, that's part of it," said Molly. She had gone to church her entire life and knew the drill. She knew what she was supposed to believe, and how she was supposed to think. But sometimes, she got a really sick feeling when she thought about it. "What about those who don't believe?" she wondered. "Are they really going to hell? Is Harriet?"

Eating her cold, dry muffin, Molly chewed and thought. After a moment, she said, "No. I can't let it go. I care about others too much to not go."

"Fine," said Harriet. "Do whatever makes you feel good." Holding up the last of her shake, she asked, "Sure you don't want a taste?"

"No," said Molly. "Definitely not. I want to fit into my swim suit this summer."

"And I won't?" laughed Harriet.

"No," said Molly. "You won't."

As much as Molly loved her friend, in this moment she wanted her to feel the pain that she felt. Hurt like she did when she thought about church, God, and all that she had been taught she was supposed to believe.

"Harriet," asked Molly during another lunch meeting, "do you believe in fate?"

"Like predetermination?"

"Yeah, like destiny."

"Well," said Harriet, "I can look at it two ways. If it's true, then I don't really have any control over my life."

"Yes," Molly nodded in agreement.

"And if it's not true," said her friend with a laugh, "then I can decide right now to get up and leave."

"Please don't," said Molly.

"Not to worry," said Harriet. "I'm still waiting for my sandwich."

"So...which do you think it is?" asked Molly.

"I don't know..."

"Who ordered the veggie club with avocado?" asked the tiny Hummingbird dragging an enormous tray.

"Me," said Harriet.

"Then the cucumber sandwiches must be yours," she said to Molly.

"Nope, mine," said Harriet. "Been trying to add more green to my diet."

"Nothing for me," said Molly to the server. "Just the shake," she said, holding a drink in her hand.

"Well," said Harriet, taking an enormous bite of her sandwich, "let me mull this over for a bit."

No one else could have possibly understood her. So muffled with food was her reply. But Molly knew her best friend so well, she could almost read her mind. But only almost. She couldn't tell what her friend was thinking about predetermination.

"Why do you ask?" said Harriet, once satiated.

"I dunno," said Molly. "Just thinking."

"You think too much," laughed Harriet. "But," she said, swallowing her cucumber sandwiches whole, "If it *is* true, as in predetermination is true, that's kind of cool too."

"How so?" asked Molly.

"Because then you can't do anything wrong. I mean, you can't get it wrong, and," she giggled, "you can't do anything about me taking your shake."

"Oh, yes I can!" said Molly, pulling it close and taking a big, final slurp. "See? It's finished. Now you can take it."

"That's what I mean!" laughed Harriet, grabbing her friend's empty shake container.

"Molly," said her mother, gently shaking her shoulder. "You need to wake up. I have something I have to tell you."

"Aw, Mom. Go away. I didn't get to bed till late," she said, pulling the covers back up over her head.

"Molly, dear," her mother said again softly. "It can't wait."

"Sure, it can," said Molly from beneath the covers.

"No," her mother said. "I need to tell you now."

There was something different about her mother's voice. A sense of urgency, but also kindness. Sympathy.

"Oh no!" Molly said, suddenly throwing back the covers and sitting up straight. "What's happened? Dad?" she asked hesitantly. Terrified of what she was going to hear, Molly's entire body began to shake violently.

"No," said her mother's shaking head, "not your father."

"Minnie?"

Again, "No."

"Then...who?"

"Molly, I just got a call from Mrs. Crossley."

And in that moment, she knew. Molly somehow knew that her best friend Harriet was gone.

"She was hit," her mother said gently. "By a truck. Molly, she didn't have a chance, she didn't..."

"No!" cried Molly as she dove deep under the covers. "It can't be. They're mistaken!" she screamed.

And yet, in every cell of her body, she knew. They weren't mistaken. It was true. She could feel it. "Harriet's gone," she sobbed.

"I'll make a cup of cocoa," her mother said, unsure of what to do. "Would you like a cup of cocoa?"

"Do I look like I want a cup of cocoa?" Molly screamed from under the covers. "Leave me alone!" she sobbed.

"Okay, dear," her mother said, getting up quietly. "I'll just leave you alone."

She did return later with cocoa. It was cold and untouched when she came back even later. "Molly," her mother said, "dinner's ready. I've made your favorite."

The quiet emanating from her daughter's bed brought a wave of shivers up and down her spine. "She's gone," thought Molly's mother. "Her best friend is gone."

"Molly, you have got to get a hold of yourself," her father said once again. He was really starting to worry about his youngest. Over a month had passed since they had learned of her friend's death. And still, Molly kept herself locked up in her room. "You can't go on like this," he gently added.

Crying, she asked, "But why Daddy? Why did she have to die?"

"I don't know, Molly. No one knows. She's in God's hands now," he said, doing his best to reassure her.

"What does that mean? In God's hands? If he's holding her, then why doesn't he just put her back where she belongs? Here on earth? With me?"

"I know you loved Harriet, Molly. I know she was your best friend. But she's gone. You need to move on."

"I want to be alone."

"Alright," he said, "I understand that you still need some time. But, Molly, you'll have to go back to school on Monday. We can't put it off any longer."

She didn't look up when he quietly shut the door and left her room.

"Why God?" she asked for the thousandth time, but still, she felt no answer.

Exhausted from her nonstop weeping, Molly gradually fell into a stupor. Which became drowsiness. And then finally, the solace she had been seeking came in the form of a deep, deep sleep. Darkness fell as the day turned to night. Time stood still. Molly simply was. Under her covers. In a never-ending blackness.

Days, weeks, or simply hours later, she heard a faint something from deep within her well. "Molly!" it called, gradually growing louder and louder. "Molly! Wake up!"

"Huh?" she asked as she fell onto the hard floor. "Ouch, that hurt!" Struggling to find her way out of her bed covers and turn on the light, she pulled herself up off the floor.

"Click." She found the switch, but the sudden brightness was too harsh. Too much. "What in the heck is going on?" she wondered as she dove back onto her bed.

"Molly!" she heard again. This time the voice was more clear.

Not so far away. "Wake up! It's about time you got up!"

"No," Molly told herself, holding the covers firmly over her head. "No. It can't be. She's gone. She got hit and died. She can't be here telling me to get up. Or...?" Slowly, with great trepidation, Molly began to push back the covers. One layer at a time. When she couldn't stand it any longer, she opened her eyes and peeked beyond the pillow she held pressed against her head.

"Hi!" waved Harriet, sitting on the other side of the room. "'Bout time you got up. Look at you. You're a mess!" she said, now standing in front of Molly, who still lay curled on her bed. "Oooo, let's wipe that drool off. What do you say, Molly? Ready to be rid of that slobber?" her friend asked lightly. "And when's the last time you took a bath? You stink!"

"Harriet?" asked Molly, barely whispering. "Is that really you?"

"Well," she said with a teasing smile, "It's not the pope."

"But, but...?" asked Molly.

"Yes," her friend replied. "I'm dead."

"Then how..."

"I couldn't leave you like this, Molly," her friend said. "Your dad's right. You've got to get a hold of yourself. Move on."

"Awww," said Molly as she once again began to cry. "How can I do that Harriet? How can I go on without you?"

"Because you can," her friend said with force. "I always told you that you were more talented than you thought. More capable than your wildest dreams. Everyone is. They're just too caught up with what they think they're supposed to be doing that they waste their life dealing with a bunch of crap that just doesn't matter. Molly," she said again softly, "you'll be alright. I know you will."

"What was it like?" asked Molly. "Dying?"

"It happened so fast. I was here one moment, and then I wasn't."

"Did it hurt?"

"No," said Harriet. "Thank God. It was so quick that I didn't feel a thing. You don't need to worry about any of that. In fact, you don't need to worry about a thing. That's what I really came here for. To tell you that."

"What?" asked Molly. She was still in such a tailspin that she wasn't sure if she was awake or dreaming. "Harriet?" she wondered. "Here with me? How is that possible?"

"Molly," her friend said once again, "you're not dreaming. I'm really here."

She too was enjoying this moment, savoring each chance she got to say her friend's name. "Mo-lly," she said slowly, "you know all that stuff we used to talk about?"

"The God stuff?" asked Molly.

"Yes," said Harriet. "I'm here to tell you that you don't need to worry about a thing. Not one little thing. *Chill out*," she added gently.

"Chill out?" asked Molly. "Chill out? But this stuff is serious? How can you just say, 'Chill out'?"

"Because I can. And because it's true. You don't have *a thing* to worry about. Not one itty bitty thing."

Molly didn't know what to say. Any question she would think of later evaporated in that moment. All that mattered was that her friend was there with her. But before Molly could take another breath, say anything further, her friend opened the door to leave. "Gotta go, Molly," she said as her body began to fade.

"Wait. Don't go!" yelled Molly desperately.

"I have to," her friend said softly. "But please, Molly, for real, relax. You don't need to worry about a thing. Ever." And with that, the door blew shut, and her best friend was gone.

You'd Make a Great Teacher
or
Adult Education

"Molly," asked Miss Peggy, "have you ever thought about becoming a nurse? I think it would suit you."

"Me?" said Molly. "No way. The thought of blood just creeps me out."

"But you told me you like biology. You could get over that blood stuff. It really wasn't so bad," said Miss Peggy, who in addition to her profession as a nurse volunteered as a camp counselor. Unlike the mountain camp Molly attended when young, this camp took place at the beach. Their church simply rented cabins for a week and turned it into their camp. Molly was so glad she had made a connection with Miss Peggy. A gentle soul, and the most adorable Goat Molly had ever seen, Miss Peggy had an open and modern outlook on life.

"I have considered going into the medical field," said Molly. "But as much as I love learning how bodies work, I can't help but twitch when the teacher starts describing...Ooo!" she squealed, grossing herself out just at the thought of someone being sliced open.

"Well," said Miss Peggy, "you're so good with the younger kids at camp. How about a teacher?"

"Hmm," thought Molly. "My dad's a teacher. A professor really. He teaches math at the college."

"I know," laughed Miss Peggy. "Everyone knows your dad."

"Yes," said Molly. "He's a flirt, that's for sure."

"True, but do you like his lifestyle? He gets a lot of time off," said Miss Peggy.

"And he really doesn't even work that much. Seems like all his assistants are doing everything for him. But...if I did, I'd want to work with the younger kids," said Molly.

"That's what I'm saying," said Miss Peggy. "I've watched you on the playground, and you're as much a kid as them."

"Great," said Molly.

"I don't mean it in a bad way," she explained. "I mean, you relate to them well. Get down on their level. And I can see that they really like you."

"You think?" asked Molly.

"I know," she said. "Some of my best friends in college are in education, and they love it."

"But I hear about all the paperwork you have to do. The Federal regulations..."

"There will always be things like that, Molly," said Miss Peggy, not letting her finish, "in any job. But if you're doing what you love, it won't ever feel like work."

"Is that how it is for you?" asked Molly. "Being a nurse?"

"Well, it's still fairly new, but, yes, I love it. I love it when I can help ease someone's pain, their suffering. And," she added with a gleam in her eye, "how else could I get hold of all these birth control devices." She then leaned down, opened the oven door, and pulled out a tray of the strangest looking gadgets Molly had never imagined. "What are they?" Molly asked. "Birth control devices," Miss Peggy repeated, "I figured that most of your parents wouldn't teach you about this, and it's something you really do need to understand."

Miss Peggy closed the oven door and turned her attention back to Molly. "Pick your jaw up off the floor, Molly!" she laughed. "It doesn't mean I'm saying go use them, but you girls do need to be aware of what they are...and how they work. You're an adult now. You need to be able to take control of your life." Then softening her tone, she added, "Now get on out of here. I've got to get ready for your class."

"Okay," Molly simply said as she left. "Wow," she thought to herself, "there's so much you have to think about when you're an adult."

The Key to Success
or
Says Who?

"We're so glad you came, Molly," said Mrs. Hare, grinning more like a Cheshire Cat than the long-eared Hare that she was.

"Thanks," said Molly, looking around. "Haven't been here since I was a foal."

"Then it's about time," Mrs. Hare said with glee. "We've been inviting you to these advanced classes for ages. How is it we got lucky this time?"

"Something was cancelled, so I thought, why not?" answered Molly truthfully.

"Well," said Mrs. Hare, clearly curious as to what had been canceled but too proper to ask, "we're sure glad it did. Aren't we?" she asked the rest of the gathering.

Faint murmurs of agreement were heard around the conference room.

"This isn't like I remember it," said Molly.

"Oh, there have been upgrades," said Mrs. Hare. Seeing that Molly was looking out the windows and up towards the cabins, she added, "The camp cabins are still up there. You can check them out later. But we needed something more civilized for us adults. Isn't this building nice?"

Molly just smiled politely. "What's the point of being in the mountains?" she thought.

"Welcome to camp," Mrs. Hare said to the entire group. "Our weekend retreat is focusing on success. What it is? And how we get there?"

Again, murmurs of acknowledgement were heard around the room.

"Having graduated from high school, all of you are now embarking on the voyage of your life. And it's important to get a good start. I'm here to give you a good shove," Mrs. Hare chuckled. "And cast you off with all that you need in order to be successful."

Polite fake laughter filled the room. There was a nervous energy throughout. Everyone felt it. Especially Molly.

"So," Mrs. Hare continued, "before we officially begin, does anyone have an idea of what being successful means?"

Molly's hoof shot straight up. She knew. She always had.

"Yes, Molly," said Mrs. Hare. "Why don't you come on up and tell us what you think."

"Well," said Molly once she reached the front, "it's easy really. Just do what you love, and the rest will take care of itself. True success is feeling at peace with yourself."

"What?" shouted someone in the back row. "That's bull malarkey. Everyone knows it's about making money. Having a good job. House. Car." Molly barely knew this Donkey, but she did know that his family owned a luxury car dealership in town.

"Well," she thought as she went back to her chair, "that went over like a lead brick. I most definitely don't fit in here."

"Quiet!" shouted Mrs. Hare. "I need for all of you to bring down the volume. We're adults here. Let's show some respect."

It took several minutes for the talking to stop. No longer a polite murmur, it was clear that Molly was the only one who considered being at peace a mark of success.

"Thank you, Molly, dear," said Mrs. Hare politely. "That was really sweet. But now we're going to talk about the real world. How you can empower yourselves to be successful in the world we live in."

The rest of the weekend, Molly was absent. Oh, she was physically present. She had made a commitment and was going to stick to it. But rather than listen to what she now realized was nonsense, she withdrew into her private world. A world where love and peace were all that mattered.

"Perhaps it's a fantasy to others," she thought, "but I know what's real. I can feel what's important."

Anytime there was a break from the official workshop, Molly was in the woods. Hiking. Exploring. Or simply thinking.

"God?" she asked. "Am I crazy? True success is being at peace, isn't it?"

She received no clear reply. Saw no thunderbolts nor heard no deep, booming voice. Instead, she experienced a calmness which arose from within herself. It reminded her of how she felt when she practiced what her best friend, Harriet, had taught her. "Focus on your heart, Molly. That's where all love comes from."

"But how is it that what Harriet taught me brings me peace?" she wondered. "And not what I've been told I'm supposed to believe?"

That weekend Molly also found the old campfire site she had visited as a young foal. Memories from that time slowly began to rise up in her mind's eye. The camp leader, Butch. Her cabin counselor, Miss Betty. The Eagle, so wise. And in that remembering came a knowing. "We're all searching for the same thing. In every trinket we buy. In every experience we have. All we're really wanting is to be at peace. Feel happy and connected to others. We've just gotten lost," Molly realized. "Forgotten that we already have what we're seeking."

"Molly!" called Mrs. Hare from the top of the hill. "Whatever are you doing down there? We've got to get going! The van's leaving in five minutes."

"Oh," thought Molly, slowly coming out of her fog of bliss. "Where am I?" she wondered. "*When* am I?" A strong feeling of déjà vu surrounded her. "This happened before," she thought. "I remember..."

But before she could remember, Mrs. Hare screamed at the top of her lungs, "Molly! Come! Now!" That screech effectively brought Molly back to earth. To the realm where life revolves around the accumulation of things. Accomplishment.

"That's my girl," said Mrs. Hare as Molly trotted up to meet her. "We'll make a success out of you yet."

Spiders, Spiders Everywhere!
or
What the?

"Drat!" yelled Molly to no one in particular. She was all alone. Her college roommates had gone shopping. So, no one was there to witness the mess she had just made. Dashing to the kitchen, she grabbed a rag and quickly cleaned it up. Long ago, Molly had resigned herself to the fact that she was a Spiller of things. All kinds of things. Her milk when she was young. Beer when at a frat party. And now, on a cold winter day – cocoa.

"I try to be careful. I really do." But no matter how careful she was, it seemed to happen at the most inopportune time. She had been just about to curl up with a good book.

"Oh well," she thought, "I'll just make another." Soon she was back in her cozy cocoon on the couch, covered with heaps of warm fuzzy blankets.

Saturdays were special to Molly. She had finished all her homework for Monday the night before. While all the other college students were out partying, Molly was home alone studying. She had done that all through college, and it had served her well. Besides having a cozy Saturday morning alone with a good book, she didn't experience the stress that everyone else complained about on Sunday nights as they crammed to complete their assignments.

Finally lost in her story, Molly could feel the gentle breeze of ancient Greece. Smell the salt air. See the ships on the horizon. And then, something crawled across her hoof. Mindlessly, she brushed it away. A few seconds later, it happened again. And then again. And again.

"What's going on?" she asked out loud, casting aside her book and many blankets with one hoof while carefully holding onto her mug with another. "Oh no you don't," she told herself. "I'm not making another." Carefully, she set the cocoa on the dining room table.

"Okay," she said, returning to the sofa, "what is going on?"

She looked where she had been comfortably reading only moments before and saw spots. Hundreds if not thousands of tiny, white spots. "They're moving," she thought. Like a white wave, they were washing across her blankets.

"What the?" asked Molly again. "I can't have lice," she thought, suddenly unable to stop scratching herself. She crouched down low and examined the blankets more closely. "What could it possibly be?"

"Spiders!" she suddenly shouted.

The white spots were Spiders. "Tiny, tiny Spiders!" she exclaimed. "And they're all coming out of that big one!" she said, realizing that the larger white spot was an egg sack. "Oh, my goodness!" Molly had never seen such a sight.

Heading straight to the window, she shoved it open. "Brrrr," she said as cold air burst inside. "You're not going to get me, Cold. You're going to get Spiders. Lots and lots of them!"

She collected all the blankets, careful to keep the egg sack in the center. "Okay, my little lovelies," she told them, "you're going outside. Time to live your little Spider lives in the great outdoors. Only college students in this apartment."

Flinging the blankets with all her might, she leaned out as far as she dared, mindful to not let go. Miniscule specks were caught in the breeze and floated through the frosty morning sky.

Once she was sure that they were all gone and that no stragglers still clung to the blanket, she came back in, lowered the window, and wrapped herself up in the now cold blankets. Giving her cocoa a short zap in the microwave, she once again snuggled on the couch. Soon Molly was lost in the warmth of ancient Greece and completely forgot about the Spiders.

Try and Relax
or
Be Love

"This treatment is tricky in the best of times," said the traveling dentist. "But with your big 'ole Mule mouth," he laughed, "I think we'll get along just fine. Hopefully there's enough room for me to work," he said, showing her his rather large bear paws. "But the thing is though," he continued, "I'm going to have to enter your mouth from the side."

"What?" asked Molly, practically falling out of her chair.

"Careful, Molly," said the assistant, a rangy Rat with a cute little nose. "I can't have you fainting on me. We'll have to strap her in Doc."

"Ewww," shivered Molly. "Do you have to?"

"If you're going to keep going limp, we do," said the Rat. "Maybe best we lay her down on the table."

"I concur," said the dentist with a growl. "Molly, dear," he said, leaning over and making eye contact, "this will be for the best."

"Okay," said Molly as she got up from the chair. "If you say so."

"That's my girl," said the dentist.

"Funny how everyone thinks I'm their girl," thought Molly as she went to the adjacent room. She stepped onto an enormous platform, practically the size of two ping pong tables, lay down, and did her best to relax. Closing her eyes, she felt guided to send the dentist love. Straight from her heart.

For the next two hours as the dentist struggled with whatever it was he had to do in order to add skin to her gums, Molly continued to surround him with love.

"Well," he said, suddenly snapping the extra-large gloves off his paws, "that was a lot easier than I expected!"

"Darn tootin'!" said the Rat, scurrying off with the tools. "Piece of cake!"

"Cake?" asked Molly, slowly lifting her focus from her heart. But before she did completely, she sent one last blast of love, as well as a wave of gratitude. "Thank you, Dentist. Thank you, God."

"You'll not be wanting to eat anything, Molly, dear," said the dentist. "For at least one day. There's a cavity on the side of your tooth about the size of a small Goat," he chuckled.

"I can't eat?"

"No dear, not until the day after next. But," he said still laughing, "the good thing is I don't think you're going to want to."

He was right. She didn't want to eat anything that day. Or the next. Or the day after. But...when she did eat, she was so hungry that she devoured three large mushroom pizzas all by herself.

Walk All Over Me
or
What's It Really About?

"You can put it there," Stan said when Molly brought his coffee. They had only been dating a few weeks, and Molly wanted to make a good impression on their first Sunday morning together.

"As you know," he said, picking up the hot mug, "mornings are very important to me. That's when I get my best work done."

"I know," said Molly. "I won't bother you a bit."

"Good," he said, taking a sip. "Aaugh, this is terrible!" he shouted, pushing the mug toward Molly. "There's way too much sugar."

"Oh, I'm so sorry! I'll make another."

"Of course, you will," he said, turning back to his work. "That's undrinkable."

A few minutes later, she brought a second mug, this time served on a tray with cream and sugar. Molly was proud of herself for finding an easy solution. "He can add as much as he wants."

"Here you go," she sang, enjoying the morning with Stan. But when she set the tray on his desk, it got bumped, and coffee spilled all over his papers.

"Oh! I'm so sorry!" said Molly, already mopping up the mess.

"How could you be so careless? I spent weeks working on this data."

"But those are printouts," said Molly. "Can't you just print them again? I mean, I'm really sorry I spilt your coffee, but you've got a printer, and it's not the end of the world..."

"What could you possibly know about any of this? Half my morning is wasted anyway," he complained.

"I'll make another," she said, thinking, "Surely that'll make him happy."

But it didn't. Nothing would. It would take Molly a long while to realize that nothing would make him happy. But still, she tried. Over and over again, she tried.

"Molly, you've got to be more careful," she told herself as she hurriedly got her things. She closed the door so softly that he didn't even notice she had left. "Well," she thought as an afterthought, "this gives me a chance to get my own work finished. Only one more paper to write, Molly, my dear," she said with a smile, "and after four years of hard work, you'll be one step closer to earning that doctorate!"

"How can I get him to stop talking about himself?" Molly asked Miss Peggy the next time they met.

"How can I get *you* to stop talking about *him*?" her mentor answered. "Molly," she continued, "do you realize that all you talk about is Stan? How brilliant he is. What a wonderful chemist he is. How he's going to solve all our problems and save the world?

Really? Can anyone be that wonderful? And if he is, then why are you always so upset when you talk about him?"

"But, but, he is wonderful, Miss Peggy," Molly gushed. "He truly is!"

"Methinks you doth protest too much," her former camp counselor and now mentor said.

"Shakespeare," said Molly. "Hamlet."

"Right. Good to see you're paying attention in class. But seriously, Molly, all you ever talk about is this boyfriend of yours. If you really need to talk, I'm happy to listen. But...don't you think about anything else? Like, what you want? What excites you? Rather than Stan said this, Stan said that?'"

"But..."

"I understand, Molly. You like the guy. But here's something I want you to think about," she said, taking a deep breath. "It's all about you. It's only ever been about you. We all do it. Focus on others. What's wrong with them. How *they're* showing up. But what we're really doing is distracting ourselves. Keeping ourselves from thinking about what's bothering us. What we're feeling in this very moment."

Molly didn't know what to say. How to respond. Miss Peggy had hit a nerve. A place in Molly that she wasn't yet ready to visit.

"I'll leave you alone with your thoughts," she said. "But, Molly, think about it. It's only ever been about you."

And So It Went
Until
It Didn't

Molly did follow her mentor's advice. She became a teacher, earning an elementary education certificate to go along with her Ph.D. in mathematics. For years she worked with young children and loved it. Until she couldn't take it any longer.

"Why are you quitting, Molly?" asked her cousin Frank, the school principal. "You do such a great job with the kids."

"Oh, I do love them," said Molly sadly. "But it's just too hard."

"Is it that new student? I can talk to his parents?"

"No, no," said Molly. "It's not that. It's just...too hard to be around them. I love children so much, and..." She couldn't bear to finish the sentence with what she was really thinking, "It just hurts too much since I can't have my own."

"Well, you don't need to make any rash decisions," he said. "You're here till the end of the year you said. Right?"

"Yes, of course. I'll finish the year," she said as she meekly left the office.

"What am I going to do?" she wondered. "I have to work, but..."

"You could adopt," her friend Betsy said when they talked on the phone later.

"Sure," said Molly. "But by myself? That wouldn't be fair to them, and I don't know if I could do it on my own."

Molly had never found Mr. Perfect, that special someone her mother had told her to hold onto, *if* she ever found him. "Definitely not Stan," Molly thought. "He hated children. Much too messy."

"Okay, class!" called Molly as she entered her classroom. "It's transition time. You'll be working on your math project next."

"Thank you, Miss White," she said to the music teacher who was gathering her things. "How did they do?"

"Great. That new student needed a little coaxing, but he'll do better next week, I think."

"Good. I'll talk to him, see if I can add support in any way. I appreciate all you do. The children love music."

"My pleasure," she replied. "But Miss Molly," she said before leaving the room, "they really couldn't wait for you to get back from your meeting. They love you so much."

But Molly did quit. Left the job that brought her so much pain.

"Remember," her former professor and now current boss told her, "this is a temporary position. Just until Professor McDonald returns."

"I understand," she replied. "I really appreciate your call. It couldn't have come at a better time."

"Well, I'm glad it worked out. It wouldn't have even occurred to me, if I hadn't seen Fred. Remember him? Your classmate from Minnesota?

"Sure," said Molly. "I ran into him a few weeks ago at the store."

"That's what he said. He also mentioned that you recently left your teaching position. And," he added with a smile, "it just so happened that Professor McDonald called the very next day saying he had to take some time off. Well," he laughed, "you sure are one lucky Mule! And you always were one of my favorite students. Happy to have you back...for however long it lasts."

"Me too," said Molly.

As the end of the semester neared, the department head called her into his office. "Can I offer you a coffee?" he asked.

"No, I'm fine," said Molly. "I can't take the chance of spilling it," she thought. "It'd keep me up all night," she explained.

"Just one coffee," he said as he buzzed his receptionist. "So, Molly," he said, "remember how I said this was a temporary position?"

"Yes," she quietly answered.

"I just got off the phone with Professor McDonald, and it just so happens that this break he needs isn't so temporary after all."

"No?" asked Molly, seeing where this could go and doing her best to not get too excited too soon.

"No, and well, the thing about it is, I need to make this a permanent position."

"Yes," said Molly, hoping it was turning in her favor.

"And, well," he said hesitantly, "I have to make it public first. I can't just call up a former student and give her a permanent position."

"Oh," said Molly, realizing that she may be out of work after all. "I see."

"Now that doesn't mean that you couldn't get it. But...you did leave the university to work with those youngins, and don't get me wrong, that was important work. I'm sure it was, but I'm not so sure the hiring board will feel the same way."

"Oh," said Molly again. "Is there anything I can do? To help persuade them? Let them know I'm good with students of all ages?"

"Well," he said thoughtfully, "all you really can do is your best work. Impress the heck out of them with the classes you have now. Make it seem like a waste of time to do an intensive search for candidates, and," he said with a wink, "I can give a little nudge now and then. Remind them how much a search will cost, that our budget is almost used up," he laughed. "I can't make any promises, Molly, but I can sure try."

"Thanks," she said, getting up to leave. "I appreciate your honesty. I'll do my best on my end."

"You can do it," she heard deep inside herself as she walked down the hall to her tiny office. "Just be yourself, and everything will work out fine."

Molly landed the position with ease – assistant math professor. She then quickly rose to full professor with tenure.

"Professor Molly," said her assistant with a quick tap at the door, "you're wanted on line two. Some big wig at the chemical plant, I think."

"What could he want?" Molly wondered.

She was enjoying her life. The security. Consistency. The comfortable groove that she had settled into. All that was about to change.

"Yes?" said Molly, picking up the phone, "This is Professor Molly."

"Why hello there, Professor. This is Bob Campbell from down at the chemical plant. Seems you've developed quite a reputation for being good with numbers."

"Oh?" Molly simply replied.

"Yes, and well," he coughed, "we need some help over here. Business is going gang busters, and we're just about to jump to the next level. But before we do that, we could sure use some outside assistance."

"That certainly is flattering," said Molly, "but I don't see how..."

"Tomorrow at two. Can you be here? At my office? We're pulling together all our biggest heads. Gonna have a brain storm."

"Well," said Molly hesitantly, "I am free, but..."

"Good, we'll see you then," he quickly replied. "Click." He had hung up.

"What was that about?" wondered Molly.

"Another call on line two," her assistant buzzed from the adjacent room. "The head of the department, this time."

"Professor Molly," she announced.

"Hi there," the department head said with gusto. "Just checking to see if Bob made contact with you."

"He did."

"Good. He's a friend of the family. A Mole of high standing. Promised him the moon and back again. Make good on my promise, you hear!" he commanded. "Click." He too hung up before Molly could ask any questions.

This fast pace became Molly's life. Her new routine. Up early to meet with other mathematicians, chemists, scientists of all sorts. Grab another coffee and then hurry on to the university where there were more meetings and classes to oversee. On and on it went. Until Molly's life became a whirling dervish. A storm of the mind.

There were some perks, however, to go with the non-stop work. "Ever been to a Super Bowl, Professor Molly?" asked Bob Campbell's young assistant after an especially long meeting. "No," she answered. "You are now!" the assistant chirped, bouncing her cute canary body all over her desk. "Fifty-yard line. And bring a friend," she added, pointing to an envelope with her beak.

After that, came checks. Lots of them. Molly was earning more money than she could possibly spend.

"Great job, Professor," Bob Campbell frequently said over the phone. "Our profits are shooting out the roof."

"Thank you," said Molly. "Glad to be of service."

And she was. Glad. Glad to have this extra work. Money. And feel needed. But in those few rare moments when quiet reigned, she could feel that something was off. Awry. Her life wasn't turning out like she had thought it would.

Please Notice Me
or
The Things We Forget

"Dad, will you please stop watching all the other players?" asked Molly for the umpteenth time.

"Sorry, Molly," her dad replied. "They're just so very interesting."

"And I'm not?" she asked, obviously hurt.

It was so rare for Molly to find a spare moment to spend with her dad that she was willing to play the game she liked least just to be with him. But every time they met at the chess league, he paid more attention to the other players than to her. It drove Molly nuts.

"Oh, of course you are," he lied. "Very, very interesting."

"Doesn't anyone tell the truth?" Molly wondered. "Maybe not," she thought, remembering the strain in her mother's angry voice, "Don't ever say what you're really thinking, Molly. You wouldn't want to be rude!"

And so, she had. Followed her mother's advice. Kept everything inside until she was about to explode. Molly had fooled herself so completely that she hadn't realized she had actually swallowed it all: hook, line, and sinker. Everything she had been taught a good girl should do.

"No, not me," she had told herself. "I'm a Feminist. I can do anything I want!"

And yet, she'd found herself in relationship after relationship where the male called the shots. Oh sure, they were polite too. They had swallowed the same pill. "What would you like to do, Molly?" they would ask. But when she told them, they would convince her that something else was much better. "Oh, you don't really want to see that movie, do you? I've heard this one is great!"

This had happened so often that by the time Molly was ready to graduate from college she had forgotten who she was. Really was. At her core.

Bob, the adorable Stallion she drooled over. Gorgeous. A hunk. But dumber than a door knob.

Stan, the brilliant chemist. So interesting to talk to. Until she realized all they talked about was him.

Phillip, the sensitive artist. So dashing with his beret. So classy. And so darn selfish.

"Why can't I ever find a nice boyfriend?" she thought. "A man, really. 'Cause all these guys are boys." She talked about it so often that friends would avoid her. "Oh, hi, Molly," they would say. And then quickly find an excuse, a reason they had to leave.

"Am I always going to be alone?" she wondered. "Or lonely with a jerk? Didn't I use to think my own thoughts? Be my own Mule?"

"Yes, Molly," a voice inside her said. "Of course."

But she ignored it. Turned away. Kept herself busy planning whatever it was she thought she was supposed to be doing. That day. The next. And the one after. Molly was such a good planner that she had everything figured out up until the day she died.

And it worked. For years. Molly, the successful teacher. Molly, the successful professor. Molly, the magical go-to for numbers. Climbing the ladder of success, she had told herself that she was simply hungry for knowledge. Glad to contribute.

And still, a voice so silent that it was easy to ignore would often say, "Molly, we love you. We know who you really are."

And then one day, her childhood friend Betsy came home for a visit. "Wow, Molly," she gushed in her typical Betsy way, "it's so cool all that you've done! You're the only mathematician I know. I mean, you're just so smart!"

"Sweet Betsy," thought Molly. "Always there to cheer one up. Even after all I did to her. I wasn't really all that nice."

"Why are you so sad?" asked Betsy suddenly.

"What? Me? I'm not sad. I, I must have been thinking about something that I have to do."

"Of course," said Betsy. "I imagine you're really busy. Having such an important job and all."

"Oh, it's not all that important."

"Sounds like it, from what I've heard. But," her friend asked, "do you enjoy it?"

"Well, of course," said Molly, without giving it much thought. "Of course," she told herself again. "Why wouldn't I?"

Betsy had known Molly for most of her life. True, they hadn't hung out much since high school, but still, she knew her friend and could tell when something was wrong.

"Do you?" asked Betsy again. "Like your job?"

"Well," said Molly, thinking of the many perks she enjoyed, "it certainly pays well."

"Okay," said Betsy. "I hear you, but the Molly I remember wasn't interested in any of that."

"No?" asked Molly, not so sure she was glad to see her friend after all. She wasn't feeling so great, and she didn't know why.

"Remember?" asked Betsy. "You used to love talking about all things philosophical," she laughed. "And I just wanted to think about my boyfriend."

Molly didn't respond. Betsy could clearly see that her friend was deep in thought.

"Molly?" Betsy asked gently. "What was it you came here to do?"

"Came here to do?" repeated Molly. "*Came here to do?*"

That simple question instantly transported Molly to another place and time. A place where she knew what she wanted. And a time so expansive that it seemed to last forever. Huge Alice in Wonderland sized playing cards fell on either side of her, and looking up, she saw them fall from above as well. "Ahh!" Molly gasped as she realized, "A house of cards! I've been living in a house of cards!"

"What?" her friend simply asked.

"A house of cards! OMG Betsy! I can't believe you asked me that. OMG. I've been living in a house of cards. And it just fell. I *saw* it They were this big!" she said, showing how far above her head they had spanned.

"Okay," said Betsy, not really sure what was going on.

"OMG!" Molly said again as the weight of this epiphany fully landed on her. "I've been living like I thought I was supposed to," she laughed, feeling a lightness she hadn't felt in years.

"Okay," said Betsy again. "Maybe we should just sit with this for a moment."

"Oh, that Betsy," Molly thought, "I never realized what a great friend she was. Is. So wise. So wonderful."

"I love you!" Molly suddenly gushed to her longtime friend. "Well," laughed Betsy, not quite sure how to respond, "where did that come from?"

"From deep inside," laughed Molly, feeling so giddy she wanted to jump for joy.

"Then why don't you?" she heard.

"Yes, why don't I?"

She immediately leapt from her chair and danced a little jig around her friend. "Happy dance!" Molly sang. "Happy dance!" waving her hooves to and fro.

"Are you alright?" Betsy asked.

"Don't you see?" said Molly with excitement. "You just reminded me of everything I'd forgotten. Everything that used to be so important to me."

"Wow," said Betsy, "I'm sorry if..."

"No," said Molly. "It's a good thing! OMG! It's all coming back. Everything. That Eagle at the campfire. Harriet's visit."

"Huh?" asked Betsy. "You mean that friend of yours who died a long time ago?"

"Yes," said Molly. "I never told anyone, but she came to see me after she died. She wanted me to know that I didn't need to worry. That everything was fine. *Is* fine. Just like it is. Oh!" Molly gushed again to her tiny friend. "I'd completely forgotten! I'd gotten so wrapped up in...in...I don't know. Life. Like I thought it was supposed to be. But, but who knows how life's supposed to be? I mean, it's different for all of us. We're all different, so how could it possibly be the same? Fit some little formula? Oh," said Molly after a few seconds of silence, "I need to sit down."

She leaned back in her chair and closed her eyes. She felt such gratitude. For Betsy. Her parents. Her siblings. For everyone she had ever known. All the work she had ever done. "Thank you, God," she silently prayed.

And then, she saw herself. From above. Working so hard. So diligently. "OMG," she thought, "I was so absorbed in my work, I didn't see anything else."

And with that came a knowing. "It was all *for* me. All of it. Everything. I wouldn't be the Mule I am today without every experience I've ever had. Wow!"

Molly felt so moved. So overcome with joy, gratitude, and love that she stayed seated. For a long while. She was so immersed within herself that she didn't notice a solitary Spider hanging by her side. Waiting. Simply *being*...a Spider.

Betsy, not knowing what else to do, joined them. She too closed her eyes and waited. Wondering what in the world was going on but noticing that she had never felt so peaceful.

"Betsy," Molly said once she opened her eyes, "Harriet was right. We don't need to worry about a thing. Not one little thing."

After I had that epiphany, literally saw a house of cards fall down all around me, I knew life would never be the same. I took a sabbatical from my job. From all my commitments. Got a van. And set off for parts unknown.

I had a lot of living to do. A lot of souls I needed to meet. 'Cause when Betsy asked me what I came here to do, I remembered. I came here to love. I simply came here to love. And in doing so, remind everyone that *they're* loved. And perfect as they are. In *every* moment.

I thank you for reading my story. For visiting some moments from my life.

I do have one favor to ask. Please be gentle with yourself. Kind to yourself. You're so very beautiful. Each and every one of you. God doesn't make mistakes. You're exactly how you need to be to be YOU. And when you realize that, accept yourself for who you are, your life will never be the same.

Until the next time, sending you all a big, BIG hug!

Love,

ILLUSTRATIONS
by
Jocelyne Champagne Shiner

Signed prints of these illustrations are available for purchase.
Contact the artist through her website: www.studiojocelyne.com.

ACKNOWLEDGEMENTS

This book has been touched by so many people,
it's a wonder you don't SEE their finger prints all over!

Normally, we never know how much our actions impact others.
I want ALL OF YOU to KNOW how MUCH you have affected me.
With your generosity. Kindness. And loving support.

Thank YOU. Thank you. THANK you!

First, I'd like to acknowledge the many **READERS** who took time
out of their busy lives to read whichever draft I sent their way.

You EACH brought something special
with your unique perspective.

• Dearest Chantal, as the FIRST reader, your guidance was
invaluable. You were always spot-on and helped steer me exactly
where I needed to go.

• Nakuma, you brought LIGHT which showed where a couple of
bridges needed to be constructed.

• Marty, your LOVE of the opening let me know I was off to a good
start.

• Shannon, your LOVE of the closing let me know Molly would be
fine. Also, you helped me know it was time to take a closer look at
the STRUCTURE as well as think about WHY Molly was being
interviewed! *LOL* Thank you!

• Beth, your questions were so very, very THOUGHT PROVOKING!
They led me down a path of even deeper meaning, for which I'm
grateful.

• Claire, you added a level of EXPERTISE which I greatly
appreciate. And...you edified some key elements thereby helping
me finish well done. ;-)

• Pepper & Kathy, thank you for being the LAST readers! Don't
worry, if we catch a typo later, no one will give you grief. ;-)

So very MANY people **HOUSED** me when I was in between campsites or just getting set up to camp.

Whether it was for one night or weeks on end, I'm so very APPRECIATIVE of your kind hospitality.

• Liz & Jim, you provided a much needed BASE CAMP. You never once asked, "Now when are you leaving?" And you didn't seem to mind when I became Tank's new house mother. And...to give me your Thule! Well, that just takes the cake. It also meant that I didn't have to toss a lifetime supply of journals on the side of the road. Thank you, thank you, thank you!

• Mom, thanks for being open to your daughter becoming a GYPSY. Are you happy now to hold a book in your hand after months of asking, "Aren't you finished yet?"

• Jan & Mark, you two were most GRACIOUS when it must have looked like I was moving in to stay. :) But not once did you ask me to leave. Or make me feel unwelcome. Thank you. It was so nice to be WARM and focus on the last major read-through.

Also, it was so great to be able to set Pegi up and get help building a bed platform! MAHALO Mark!

Sisters, you are always so very, very GENEROUS!

• Hannah & Dwight, the two of you lent me just what I needed when I was making my tiny, tiny, tiny van a home – a sewing machine! It was so wonderful to be able to make a space not much bigger than a coffin a comfy-cozy home. THANKS!

• Chantal & Ranga, OMG, I'd never before heard of an Indian Lemon blessing for a new vehicle, but I'm glad I have now! I felt your LOVE with me always as I was on my own hero's journey.

Dearest Reader, if you're wondering what I'm talking about, look on my YouTube channel for a VERY short video I made called: Nissan NV 200 cargo van/mini-camper.

• Katie, even though I BROKE A DISH am I welcome to return????? Your home's darling, btw. :)

• Vicki, Brad & Caroline, I can't believe 30 years flew by in what felt like two! It was so wonderful to catch up, AND the FLOSS you gave me lasted for months! Thank you!

• Helen & Rich, what an honor it was to spend time with you, visit and get to know your family farm *and* CELEBRATE Julie's life. <3

• Jocelyne & Mike, OMG, where to begin? "We're heading to Phoenix for a gig; wanna come?" That fun trip and awesome time was a precursor for the SOUL SERVING interaction and collaboration I'd get to experience with you later, Jocelyne. Mahalo Ke Akua.

• Bevin, okay, I know I didn't stay with you Bevin, but your, "Are you stopping at Winslow, Arizona and have you heard of Acoma Sky City?" couldn't have come at a more perfect time. THANK YOU!

• Sharon & Ken, how can I express my gratitude? Your kind welcome after such a long drive across the desert warmed the cockles of my heart. It was also such a treat to spend the evening with you and your guest. I love how your home is a HAVEN for so many travelers.

• Dear Tanya, Thor, Tristan & Sienna, WOW! To join up with friends from Kauaʻi, hang out on their boat, laugh and watch YouTube videos...it just doesn't get any better than that!

• Precious Timi & Ed, just being with you both was such a JOY!And Timi, your, "Sweetie, do you see those clouds? That's from the fire along the coast. I'm concerned about the air quality if you go camping now." Some of these stories I wrote in your loving home as I waited for the air to clear. :)

• Claire & Paul, you live in HUMMINGBIRD HEAVEN! I loved it! Spending time with you is always "da best."

• Donna, my new sister of the HEART, how grateful I was to have a safe haven from the fires AND a place to spread out the many stories I'd written (for this book) and see how they FIT together!

• Sherry & Dana, not only did you house me and feed me, you CLOTHED me! *LOL* How lucky am I to carry your mana with me in the very clothing I wear. Mahalo.

The following is a list of people who gave **LOVING SUPPORT** in one way or another. Mahalo!

- Janine (LOVE you! <3)
- Jim at Lowe's
- Nancy at B.B. & B.
- Chris & Casey
- Tank (LOVED the many walks ;-)
- Erin from SB
- Dayton & Sheila (LOVE first :)
- Grace & Beau (Big Sur by way of NY & Miami)
- Maddy from Santa Cruz (and now in Costa Rica???)
- Jonathan from SB (Eastside Library)
- Ace & Sal from SB
- Ojai librarians
- Ojai Film Festival
- Ojai WordFest
- Eva & Duncan (Thanks for breakfast and all your writing advice!)
- Mike from SB (Estatic Dance ;-)

- Judy from Ojai (It was such a pleasure to spend time with you! Mahalo for breakfast!)
- Duncan from Ojai (Thanks for lending your drill and pointing out where the Krotona library was!)
- Sergio, Alex & Erin from SB
- Valli (Mahalo for bringing Molly to LIFE!!!)
- Katie (Mahalo my longtime sister of the HEART. Your generosity is such a BLESSING.)
- Lisa (LOVE your common sense and practical tips!)
- Melissa (Punctuation Queen!)
- Lihue librarians (Your many KINDNESSES were such a gift.)
- Austin & friends <3 (Thanks for being the SPARK needed to bring the last drawing to life! Mahalo nui loa.)

And last, but most certainly NOT LEAST:
JOCELYNE, ILLUSTRATOR EXTRAORDINAIRE!!!

Dearest Jocelyne,
Your illustrations brought Molly and her friends and family to
LIFE!
I love how you GOT her, understood the story and helped make it
REAL.
Many, many thanks!
* Sj *

If you're looking for your name and don't see it, please know that it's written in my heart; I simply forgot to jot it down in my notes.

I appreciate EACH and EVERY ONE of YOU!

ABOUT THE AUTHOR

Sj is a free spirit who has a loving heart for all beings. She happily calls wherever she is *home*.

This is her first book though there are piles and piles of books that she's written which others simply call *Journals*.

A lover of language and travel, Sj expects many more books to arise out of the mist in her mind. "I'll keep showing up," she recently told a friend. "I'll just keep showing up and see what comes."

Stay up-to-date with Sj through her blog and website:
www.sjlehoven.com.

ABOUT THE ILLUSTRATOR

Jocelyne has been drawing her entire life.

Even a daydreaming doodle sketched while listening to a boring history lesson was beautiful and rich in detail.

An eclectic artist, she has a very wide range. Sculpture. Water Color. Illustrations. Jocelyne masters them all.

Visit Jocelyne at www.studiojocelyne.com.

Printed in Great Britain
by Amazon